## Sluggers

NAME: WILLOW WATERS
NICKNAME: "WOODY"
POSITION: RIGHT FIELDER
BATS: RIGHT
THROWS: RIGHT
PLACE IN LINEUP: THIRD
AGE: 32
BORN: AUGUST 31, 1866
HOMETOWN: PITTSBURGH, PA

Woody is the best hitter on the team, and throws the ball harder than anyone else on the Travelin' Nine. When he leaves the field, Woody always jogs in backward because he can't bear to turn his back on the game.

Illustrations © Loren Long

---

## Sluggers

NAME: LANCE ADAMS
NICKNAME: "PROFESSOR LANCE"
POSITION: FIRST BASEMAN
(USED TO PLAY THIRD BASE)
BATS: LEFT (USED TO BAT RIGHT)
THROWS: RIGHT (CAN ALSO THROW LEFT)
PLACE IN LINEUP: FIFTH
AGE: 35
BORN: SEPTEMBER 8, 1863
HOMETOWN: FINDLAY, OH

A historian at heart, Professor Lance knows all about America and its history. He lost his left eye during the war, but it has only made him a better ball player. He switched from third to first base so he could see the field better, bats left instead of right, and throws both ways depending on his whim.

Illustrations © Loren Long

---

## Sluggers

NAME: HAPPY HOOVER
NICKNAME: NONE
POSITION: PITCHER (OR HURLER)
BATS: RIGHT
THROWS: RIGHT
PLACE IN LINEUP: NINTH
AGE: 59
BORN: NOVEMBER 20, 1839
HOMETOWN: CHICAGO, IL
(NOW CALLS NEW ORLEANS, LA, HOME)

Happy is the team's pitcher and therefore the anchor of the team. The oldest player, he is respected for his showmanship on the mound and, despite his name, he never wears a smile. He feels his missing middle finger gives his fastball extra movement.

Illustrations © Loren Long

# GREAT BALLS OF FIRE

Read the other books in the Sluggers series:

MAGIC IN THE OUTFIELD
HORSIN' AROUND

**#3**

# GREAT BALLS OF FIRE

## LOREN LONG & PHIL BILDNER

ALADDIN PAPERBACKS
NEW YORK   LONDON   TORONTO   SYDNEY

ALADDIN PAPERBACKS
An imprint of Simon & Schuster Children's Publishing Division
1230 Avenue of the Americas, New York, NY 10020
Text copyright © 2008 by Phil Bildner
Illustrations copyright © 2008 by Loren Long
All rights reserved, including the right of reproduction in whole
or in part in any form.
ALADDIN PAPERBACKS, SLUGGERS, and related logo are registered
trademarks of Simon & Schuster, Inc.
Also available in a Simon & Schuster Books for Young Readers
hardcover edition, originally published as Barnstormers: Game 3 in 2008.
The text of this book was set in Century 731 BT.
Manufactured in the United States of America
First Aladdin Paperbacks edition April 2009
2 4 6 8 10 9 7 5 3 1
Library of Congress Control Number 2008939881
ISBN-13: 978-1-4169-1889-9 (pbk)
ISBN-10: 1-4169-1889-2 (pbk)

To Ernie Banks,
David Halberstam,
Rick Reilly,
Ryne Sandberg,
Dr. Harold Seymour,
and all the other
believers in baseball
and keepers of the game.
—P. B.

To my father,
William G. Long,
who introduced me
to the Big Red Machine.
I'd still rather go to a ball game
with you than anyone.
—L. L.

# Contents

# 1

★

## By the Turn of the Century

 **lizabeth Payne** braced herself against the table and looked from Griffith to Ruby. She rocked and swayed with the train as it rumbled up the tracks toward Chicago.

"We can handle it, Mom," Griffith said, staring at the lines on her forehead and around her eyes. They hadn't always been that deep.

"We're ready," Ruby added.

"Very well." Elizabeth let out a long breath. "This is what your Uncle Owen said to me the night of Daddy's funeral."

Griffith nodded. His mother didn't want to have this conversation. She was stalling, doing whatever she possibly could to avoid starting the talk.

He peeked over at Ruby. Griffith had asked that she be here, and he had been surprised at how little his mother had resisted his request. Only Graham was excluded; their little brother was sound asleep.

"He told me about this debt," Elizabeth began. "A substantial debt. One he said your father incurred."

"Ten thousand dollars," Ruby said.

"Yes," Elizabeth replied, tracing a finger along the edge of the table. "As you know, last year, when they returned from the war, Daddy brought his brother into his furniture business, since, with only one leg, Owen could no longer work on his own. Your father did what any brother would have done." She exhaled deeply again. "At around that time, Owen said they were presented with a business opportunity, some joint venture that involved limited risk. Owen claimed it would have provided us all with a level of comfort beyond our dreams."

Griffith chewed on the inside of his cheek. He had heard all this before. Not only from his mother, but also from some of the Travelin' Nine, the band of baseballers with whom they were touring the country.

His eyes wandered around the cabin. He still couldn't believe he was traveling in a Pullman Palace. Chandeliers hung from the ceiling, lamps with silk shades sat upon each table, and the entire car had electricity and a cooling system. Later, when he, Ruby, and their mother slipped back into the separate sleeping quarters in the next car, where Graham already was, they would each have their own bed.

Happy had arranged for the first-class travel. When the barnstormers had arrived at the depot back in Louisville, Happy had run into an old train buddy, a conductor on this route. He'd told Happy that a group of vacationers had missed their train connection, and that several seats, as well as a couple of sleeping compartments, had become available.

The Travelin' Nine could never afford such fancy accommodations, but Happy's friend also happened to be a baseball fan. In exchange for a handful of tickets to the game in Chicago, he'd agreed to let the entire group ride in style.

So in the next car, Doc, Bubbles, Tales, and Happy had piled into the tiny room with the two bunk beds. The other four ballists slept in the cozy seats just outside the other compartment, the one in which Graham slept.

"I didn't believe what Uncle Owen was

4

saying," Elizabeth continued. She spoke with her hand pressed firmly to her chest. "Not all of it. Your father would never have kept something like that from me. He would never have borrowed that kind of money, and if he had, he would have said so. Your father was not a speculator."

Griffith and Ruby glanced at each other. "Speculator" was a word they had both heard their father use when describing Uncle Owen. Uncle Owen liked to gamble;

he was a risk taker. He had been like that before the war, and from what their father had told them, he had been like that in Cuba as well.

Guy Payne, on the other hand, was always careful with money. Griffith and Ruby often heard others refer to their father as a "shrewd entrepreneur" with a "banker's acumen" when they visited the shop and warehouse.

"They were supposed to have had years to repay the loan," Elizabeth went on, "but when your father passed, Uncle Owen said the bank changed the conditions and requested its money by the turn of the century."

Elizabeth faced the window and ran her hand back and forth across her chest. "There is no bank." She spoke to the forests and fields passing in the night. "I know I told you the money was owed to one back in Louisville, but after saying it out loud, I realized there can't be. There's no note. There are no papers. And no bank would alter the terms of a loan in such a manner." She shook her head. "I should have known all along. The entire time your Uncle Owen spoke to me, he was rubbing his stump. He'd wheeled around to the far side of the table to try to hide what he was doing. But I saw."

Uncle Owen always rubbed the place where his leg used to be when he was nervous or unsettled. Everyone knew that.

Griffith sighed. His mother was right. Uncle Owen didn't owe money to a bank, and Griffith was almost certain he knew who was owed that money: the Chancellor.

He opened his mouth to tell her, but before he could form the words, he recalled what she had said after the game in Louisville, when he had told her he believed they were being followed by the Chancellor: *Don't ever say such a thing.*

Even though his mother now realized Uncle Owen owed money to others, Griffith still wouldn't say *his* name in front of her again. Not yet.

But Griffith was more convinced than ever that the Chancellor was behind all of this. And he also thought this was about far more than money. It was about their baseball, and—he couldn't shake the feeling—it was also about Graham.

"When he told me your father owed ten thousand dollars," Elizabeth explained, turning back to Griffith and Ruby, "that's when you heard us arguing. I'm sure the whole neighborhood heard us."

"You said, 'How are we supposed to come up with that kind of money?'" Ruby repeated their mother's words from that evening five weeks earlier. "'We never had that much money in our life.'"

Elizabeth nodded. She removed her hand

from her chest and reached across the table. She took Griffith's hand and placed it atop Ruby's hand. Then she held them both.

"Uncle Owen kept insisting there needed to be a way to get the money. He said if we didn't, it would destroy our family." Her voice cracked. She squeezed their hands. "I didn't understand what he was saying, but then he said . . . he said . . . if the money wasn't repaid, I could lose you children."

# 2

★

## On a Midnight Train

**riffith rubbed** his eyes and rolled the back of his neck along the plush upholstery of his seat. It didn't matter how luxurious the Pullman Palace was. He could never get used to riding the rails. His stomach constantly churned from the rocking and shaking, and his head throbbed from the clanking and rattling.

Lying in bed was out of the question. That made the nausea worse. So he sat by himself, a few rows down from where Scribe and Woody slept and across from his family's sleeping quarters.

He stood up. Whenever Griffith sat for too long, the queasiness became unbearable. He needed to be moving.

Walking through the car, he passed the sleeping ballists and other passengers. At the compartment where his sister, brother, and mother slept, he strummed his fingers along the wooden pocket door's latch but didn't go in.

When he reached the end, he glanced at the sign warning of the danger of crossing from car to car without a member of the crew. But Griffith had become quite adept at it. He turned the knob, opened the door, and measured the gap with his eyes. This time, it was only a few inches. Focusing on his feet and the floorboards, he stepped quickly and carefully, using the sides of the cabin for balance.

As he headed through the next car, filled

with sleeping passengers on both sides of the narrow aisle, the train jolted to the left. He braced himself on a seat, narrowly avoiding falling into the lap of an elderly woman.

Griffith couldn't wait for Chicago. And not just because it meant he would finally be able to get off the train. At first light, he would be out pounding the pavement, passing out flyers and promoting the Travelin' Nine's next game. With their dramatic victory back in Louisville, the barnstorming baseballers had earned some of the desperately needed money. But they still had so much more to go.

Griffith reached the end of the car and, once again, carefully crossed over. But when he pushed open the door, he bumped into another passenger who was blocking the aisle. It surprised Griffith. Until now, he hadn't seen anyone else awake.

"Excuse me," Griffith said without looking up.

The man didn't move.

Griffith raised his eyes. They stopped when they reached the pink handkerchief sticking out of the man's jacket pocket.

"I believe you have something," the man said.

Griffith didn't respond.

"Did you hear me? I said, I believe you have something."

Griffith peeked at the man's face, and when he saw the crooked smile, he froze. Without a doubt, the man was one of the two he had seen after the game in Louisville. It was the closest he had ever stood to one of the Chancellor's men.

Suddenly, the man reached down, grabbed Griffith by the collar, and pinned him against the wall.

"He wants what you have," the man said,

"He wants what you have."

his face so close that Griffith could smell the tobacco on his breath. "And he always gets what he wants. Always."

Then, just as quickly as he had grabbed Griffith, the man let go. He sauntered down the aisle and disappeared into the next car.

Griffith slumped to the floor.

*Beware the Chancellor.*

Uncle Owen's warning flashed into his mind. So did the tattered and bloodstained condition of the letter that contained the dire words. Griffith swallowed. The Chancellor and his men had done something to Uncle Owen. Uncle Owen couldn't possibly defend himself against them. Had they hurt him? Could the Chancellor and his men have *taken* Uncle Owen? Could they be holding him against his will?

Griffith began to tremble. At that moment, he realized his mother knew that the Chancellor was behind this. Even though she had dismissed the thought back in Louisville, she had to know. And Griffith understood why she had denied it. Either she was too terrified to admit it to herself. Or it was something a mother *never* told her children.

Even if it was the truth.

# 3

★

## *Run!*

**ho always** gets what he wants?" Ruby asked. She stood with her brother in the center of Jackson Park, where they were promoting the upcoming game.

"The Chancellor," Griffith replied. His words sounded cold as they left his lips, and he could tell they frightened her even more than their mother's had on the train. But Griffith had promised not to keep any secrets from her, no matter how terrifying.

"What do we have?"

"He must know we have the baseball. He must . . ."

Griffith stopped. Out of the corner of his eye, he spotted the men standing along the edge of the plaza. Griffith realized he and Ruby had allowed themselves to get separated from Happy and the Professor. Immersed in their conversation, they had wandered away. Griffith clenched his fist and pounded his leg. How could he have been so careless?

"Griff, what is it?" Ruby asked.

Before he had a chance to answer, he saw the men again. Only this time, they stood on the *other* side of the plaza. How did they get there so quickly? They were closer, too, and Griffith was now able to see that these were the same two men he had seen in Louisville.

Griffith clenched his fist even tighter. Was the Chancellor with his men? Had he followed them to Chicago?

At least the baseball wasn't with them. Both he and Ruby had thought it would be safer if they didn't carry it while they were promoting the game.

Ruby had found the perfect spot to hide it temporarily. She'd buried it in the bottom of the inside pocket of their mother's bag, the one in which she always stored a spare change of clothes. Ruby and Griffith knew their mother kept a very close eye on the bag, especially when she took it to the ball field. That's where she was now, with Graham, practicing with the other barnstormers. Ruby and Griffith also knew their mother would never look in that pocket.

*Smash!*

With one eye on the lookout for the Chancellor's men, and the other eye keeping watch of his sister, Griffith didn't see the large woman until it was too late. Charging through the plaza like a runaway freight train, she barreled over him, knocking him to the ground and the stack of advertisements from his grasp.

While raking in the scattered papers, Griffith's hands happened upon a pair of bare feet. They were filthy with caked-on mud around the ankles and heels, and crusted dirt between the toes. As Griffith slowly rose, he saw grass-stained trousers, a partially torn and oversize shirt, and then a long beard, white and gray. Finally, Griffith stood face to face with the old man and looked directly into his eyes, each one a *different* color.

"Run!" he shouted to his sister.

"What's the matter?"

"C'mon!" He grabbed Ruby by the arm and took off. The flyers in her hand soared into the air like confetti.

"What is it?" she cried.

"Whatever you do," Griffith shouted without looking back, "don't stop!"

"But where to?" Ruby called without breaking stride.

"Toward the fountain!" Griffith pointed.

They charged through the maze of

people in front of the Palace of the Arts
and tore past the fruit and vegetable carts
lining the North Pond. As soon as they
reached the Midway Plaisance—the area
where they had entered the park a short
time ago—they spotted Happy and the
Professor and stopped.

"You okay?" Griffith asked between pants.
He placed both hands on his knees.

"Are you?" she asked back.

Griffith nodded.

"What was that all about?" Ruby reached
over and rested a hand on her older brother's
shoulder.

"Someone was watching us." Griffith
didn't look up.

Ruby felt the hairs on her arms tingle.
"The Chancellor?"

"His men. The same ones I've seen before.
And . . ." Griffith stopped.

"And what?"

"There was this other man." Griffith stood back up.

"Who? What other man?"

Griffith paused. "He was old. And filthy. He wasn't wearing any shoes, either."

Ruby eyed him.

Griffith nodded. "Ruby, I don't think we needed to run."

"You're confusing me."

He paused again. "Now that I think about it, there wasn't anything frightening about him. Nothing at all."

"How can you be so sure?" Ruby asked, glancing in the direction of Happy and Professor Lance. The Travelin' Nine's hurler and their eye-patch-wearing first sack man remained only steps away.

"His eyes told me."

"His eyes?"

Griffith made circles with his finger and thumb in front of his eyes. "He wore these

**HURLER:**
*pitcher.*

**FIRST SACK MAN:**
*first baseman. The second baseman was often called the "second sack man," and the third baseman was often called the "third sack man."*

23

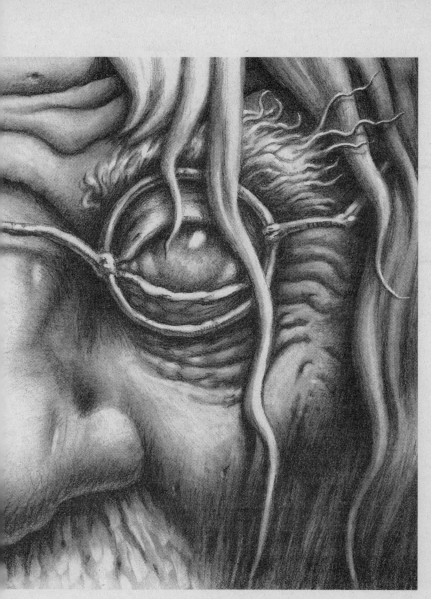

"His eyes were different colors."

round, wire-rimmed glasses. And there was a crease—a wrinkle—across the bridge of his nose. It made him look gentle, even though his eyes were different colors."

"Different colors?" Ruby raised an eyebrow.

"One was clouded over and milky white. And the other was this brilliant, twinkling blue. Like yours."

Ruby shook her head once. Then she pointed toward the two ballists. "Griff, I'm going to start handing out the flyers again, but I'm standing next to the Professor."

"I'll go keep Happy company. He looks like he could use some."

# 4

★

## Happy's Chicago

**appy was struggling.**
Standing near the end of
the Midway Plaisance,
he looked as bad as he had at the end of the
game in Louisville. He winced and grimaced,
and every so often, he would place his head
in his hands and massage his temples with
his thumbs.

Griffith sighed. Worrying about Happy
made promoting the contest against the
Chicago Nine difficult. He would hold the
flyers out to passersby, but instead of making eye contact or initiating conversation, he

found himself unable to turn away from the Travelin' Nine's hurler.

Griffith looked at the stack of papers in his hand and felt the still-stuffed satchel that he had taken from Happy to lighten his load. He peered over at Ruby and the Professor; the bag the Professor held was equally full. Griffith glanced to Happy one more time. No matter how bad the old-timer may have felt, Griffith knew he would never rest on his own.

So Griffith decided to take the lead.

"Happy, can we take five?"

"You tired?"

"A little," Griffith fibbed, motioning to an empty bench.

"Sure thing," Happy replied. "I suppose these legs of mine could use a break as well."

From the moment they left the inn, Griffith had noticed that something wasn't right with Happy. Walking to the station, Happy had clutched his side, and then on the train, he didn't say much of anything, which was very un–Happy-like.

When they had entered the park, he had lagged behind. Even after Griffith had taken the heavy satchel of advertisements from him, Happy still couldn't keep up. Griffith could see that Happy was pushing himself too hard. Like he always did.

Happy was a warrior, a soldier who never gave up. Griffith's father had shared many tales from the war about how men half Happy's age couldn't keep up with him, and how if ever anyone complained about the heat or the distance he had to cover, Happy instantly silenced the complaints.

"I'm old enough to be your father," he liked to say. "Heck, I'm old enough to be your grandfather! You don't hear a word out of me. We have a war to win."

During that war, many soldiers had contracted typhoid or yellow fever. Happy had come down with both, and since he was older than most of the servicemen, it affected him differently. It weakened his heart.

For many months after the war, Happy had been unable to work. His doctor had wanted him to retire, but Happy couldn't fathom a life not riding the rails.

Griffith and Happy crossed the pathway and sat down.

"It must feel good coming back home," Griffith said, propping his legs atop the satchel.

"Son, it always feels good coming back to Chicagoland." Happy hunched forward and rested his elbows on his knees. "But for the last few years, I've been stationed out of New Orleans, except for during the war, of course. I call the Big Easy home these days. I don't get back here much anymore. This isn't the same Chicago I once knew."

"What's so different about it?"

"Where do I begin?" Happy laughed. "The last time I was here was for the fair back in '93." He sat back up and wiped the sweat from his brow with a forearm. "Without a doubt, the single greatest moment in the history of the Windy City. Proved to the world Chicago was back."

"Back?"

"Back from the worst fire that anyone who's walked this earth has ever seen. The Great Fire of 1871." Happy paused. "I was just a boy at the time. Thirty-one years old."

"Thirty-one's not a boy. That's old!"

Happy laughed again. "Son, when you get to be my age, trust me, thirty-one is still a boy." He rested a hand on Griffith's shoulder. "I remember how old I was because that's how long the fire lasted. Thirty-one hours. Thirty-one and thirty-one. Never saw so much devastation in my entire life. Burned the city to the ground."

"This isn't the same Chicago I once knew."

"The whole city?"

"Pretty much. Most of the downtown, anyway. And to think, it was all started by a cow."

"A what?"

Happy smiled. "Son, in this town, all you need to remember is one thing: Beware the cow that kicks." Happy hoisted himself up and picked the satchel up off the ground. "Come on. I'll tell you all about the Great Fire." He pulled out a stack of flyers. "But we still have plenty of work to do."

# 5

★

## Preacher Wil

**uby felt eyes watch-**ing her from behind. She clutched the stack of flyers tightly to her chest and felt the hairs on her arms start to tingle.

How had she allowed herself to get separated from the Professor? All she had done was take a couple steps over to the boulder. Or so she thought. But when she had glanced back, the Professor was nowhere to be found in the sea of people. Ruby had never realized how quickly one could get lost in a crowd.

Now Ruby didn't dare turn around. Who

was behind her? Was it the same old man Griffith had seen only moments ago? Or was it *him*?

Instinctively, Ruby slid her hand into her pocket. Nothing. Her heart skipped a beat, but then she remembered the baseball was safely stowed in their mother's bag.

She exhaled a long breath. She wanted to call out to the Professor. She wanted to scream for Griffith. She wanted to run away as fast as she could. However, her fear wouldn't allow her to do any of those things.

So instead, Ruby said a short, silent prayer and immersed herself in the words on the bronze plaque on the boulder in front of her.

WELCOME TO JACKSON PARK
SITE OF THE WORLD'S COLUMBIAN EXPOSITION
MAY 1, 1893–OCTOBER 30, 1893

ON THIS MAJESTIC SITE ALONG THE SHORES OF LAKE MICHIGAN, THE CITY OF CHICAGO WELCOMED VISITORS FROM ALL OVER THE GLOBE TO THE WORLD'S COLUMBIAN EXPOSITION. ONLY THE WINDY CITY COULD HAVE HOSTED SUCH A GRAND CELEBRATION AND REFLECTION OF AMERICAN POWER AND VALUES, THE ONCE-IN-A-LIFETIME GALA COMMEMORATION OF THE 400TH ANNIVERSARY OF COLUMBUS'S ARRIVAL TO THE NEW WORLD.

OVER THE COURSE OF SIX MONTHS, MORE THAN 27,000,000 AMERICANS AND FOREIGNERS DESCENDED UPON THE 633 ACRES OF JACKSON PARK AND EXPERIENCED EXPO '93, THE GREATEST CULTURAL AND ENTERTAINMENT EVENT IN THE HISTORY OF THE WORLD.

Ruby lifted her head. The person watching her stood closer now.

"Everything all right, angel?"

Slowly, Ruby turned around. The tall, dark-skinned man wasn't the person Griffith had seen. And he certainly wasn't the Chancellor or any of his men.

She glanced at the dog with the grayish white coat and the black spots seated next to and slightly behind the man. The short-haired hound's snoot nestled against his leg in such a way that the dog seemed to be smiling. An answering smile crept onto Ruby's face. Her fears vanished and she suddenly felt safe, as she used to when her father would hold her during middle-of-the-night thunderstorms.

Ruby passed the man a flyer.

"What's this?" he asked, looking down at the paper.

"A baseball game," Ruby replied.

"I believe I've heard of these gentlemen."

Her fears vanished . . .

He tapped the flyer with his extra-long fingers.

"Really?" Ruby peered into the man's soft eyes as he read.

"Indeed. They recently played a match in the River City, yes?"

"Louisville!" Ruby's eyes widened. "That's right."

"These Travelin' Nine," the man said, stroking his cheek, "they friends of yours?"

"Yes," Ruby replied. "Are you a ballist?"

The man smiled, a soothing smile that matched his eyes. "Name's Wil, but folks call me Preacher."

"Nice to meet you, Preacher Wil."

"Pleasure's all mine." He tapped the flyer again. "I used to play baseball—outfield, first bag, and even a little pitcher. No more, though."

Ruby stared at Preacher Wil's left hand. Even though it was missing a finger, it reminded her of her father's hands—rugged, strong, and seemingly holding a thousand stories.

**MATCH:**
*baseball game
or contest.*

**BAG:**
*base.
Also called
"sack" (see
page 46).*

"Were you a good player?" she asked.

"What do you mean *were*?" Preacher Wil's smile widened. "I learned the game as a young'un. Wasn't much older than you, I might add. A Confederate soldier taught me baseball during our Civil War."

"The Travelin' Nine were soldiers. They were Rough Riders under Colonel Roosevelt. Are you a veteran also?"

"Not exactly, angel." Preacher Wil stroked his cheek again, and for a moment, his eyes held a faraway gaze. "I grew up in South Car'lina."

"You can't be a veteran if you're from South Carolina?"

"'Course there are veterans from the Palmetto State." Preacher Wil laughed.

Ruby shivered again. His deep bellow reminded her of her father's too.

"As a young'un," Preacher Wil continued, "that soldier told me he'd never seen anyone throw a ball as far or as fast as I could."

"Then how come you don't play?" Ruby asked, but before he could respond, a glistening object dangling from Preacher Wil's neck caught her eye. "What's that?"

"Angel, you sure ask a lot of questions."

"My daddy used to tell me the same thing."

"Got this from that same soldier," Preacher Wil said, untucking the thimble-size charm from beneath his collar. He twirled it in his fingers. "I've worn this ever since the day he placed it in my hand."

Ruby inched closer. "What is it?"

"Angel, this here I keep close to my heart. Reminds me of my purpose. Not that I need a reminder." He tucked the item back under his collar before she'd been able to see its shape, and patted his chest. "Everyone has a purpose, and mine is to help and—"

"Everything all right, Ruby?" Griffith suddenly appeared, shouldering his way through the crowd.

"Everything's fine, Griffy," she replied. "This is Preacher Wil."

Preacher Wil reached out his hand. "Nice to meet you."

Ruby looked at her brother. She saw the way he tilted his head ever so slightly and how the corners of his mouth hinted upward. Like Ruby, Griffith realized the dark-skinned man was not a threat.

He shook Preacher Wil's hand firmly. "Nice to meet you too, sir."

Griffith knelt down and held the back of his hand out to the dog still seated alongside Preacher Wil. The hound's long, floppy ears perked up as it sniffed and then licked Griffith's fingers. Griffith smiled.

Preacher Wil looked at Ruby. "I must be off now. But I have a feeling our paths will cross again." He waved the flyer once and slipped it into his front pocket. "Maybe at this park again. Or perhaps even at your game."

WEDNESDAY, AUGUST 16, 1899

# Base Ball by the Lake

*Fresh from a*

# GLORIOUS VICTORY

*in Louisville, the*

# TRAVELIN' NINE

*have blown into the* WINDY CITY.

Will they get BLOWN AWAY by the

# CHICAGO NINE?

## COME SEE for YOURSELF!

# FREE

*CRACKER JACKS & WRIGLEY'S CHEWING GUM!*

## ROUSING MUSIC & OTHER SURPRISES!

### 🖝 BUSINESSMAN'S SPECIAL 🖝

*Pregame Entertainment: Twelve o'Clock. First Pitch: One o'Clock.*

## ADMISSION 25¢. CHILDREN 10¢.

*What a*

# WONDERFUL

*way to spend a WEDNESDAY!*

# 6

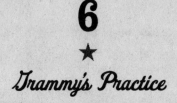

★

## *Grammy's Practice*

**G**raham stepped in front of third sack and smoothed out the dirt with his foot, first with his toe, followed by his instep. So far, he had fielded every ball cleanly, and each of his throws to Tales over at second and to Doc Lindy across the diamond at first had been right on target.

All afternoon, Graham had chased after the long hits and overthrows, helping out the Travelin' Nine. Since the Professor and Happy were downtown with Ruby and

**SACK:**
base. Also called "bag" (see page 40).

**DIAMOND:**
the infield.

Griffith, the team was short players and needed assistance. He knew if he did a good job, they would give him a chance to play at the close of practice. It was the reason he had stayed behind in the first place.

Graham reached down and flicked aside a few rocks and tossed away a handful of pebbles. He pounded his glove with his fist and rested his hands above his knees, just like Doc did prior to every pitch when he played the hot corner. The tips of Graham's fingers brushed the baseball he held in the pocket of his pants.

**HOT CORNER:** *third base.*

Before leaving for downtown, Ruby had slipped it into their mother's clothing bag, but she hadn't realized that Graham had seen her put it there. Graham retrieved the ball as soon as she and Griffith had headed out. He wanted to hold on to it for a change, and it would be just as safe with him. He would return it to the bag after practice, at the inn, before his sister and brother came back; they would never know that he had borrowed it.

"Here it comes," Woody announced with a point of the bat. "I reckon let's see what you can do with this one."

"Bring it," Graham whispered under his breath.

Woody smoked a wicked daisy cutter down the third base line.

Graham lunged to his right. Fully extended in the air behind the bag, he

**DAISY CUTTER:** *ground ball. Also known as "grass clipper" (see page 51).*

snagged the pill and then crashed to the turf. He bounced up, and then *from his knees*, he fired a frozen rope across the infield. It landed in the center of Doc Lindy's glove with a soft pop.

"Doc who?" Graham said, grinning from ear to ear. He waved to the Travelin' Nine's usual third sack man, who had shifted over to his old position so that Graham could try his hand at third.

As Graham dusted the dirt off his clothes, he looked to his mother, standing to the side of Woody behind home dish. Graham knew it was really his mother who was *letting* him play now, and the only reason she allowed him was because there was no one else in the park. He didn't quite understand why that mattered, but he didn't care. He waved to her.

"Let's see you get this one!" Woody shouted, without giving Graham a chance to set himself.

**PILL:**
*baseball. Also called "rock" (see page 55) or "rawhide" (see page 132).*

**FROZEN ROPE:**
*hard line drive or throw.*

**DISH:**
*home plate.*

The one-hop smash came directly at him, but Graham stood firm. He smothered the screamer in his midsection, even as the force of the hit lifted him off the ground. Graham regained his footing, and then, *from his heels*, unleashed a rocket across the diamond. Doc stretched for the perfect pea.

*Pop!*

"Doc who?" Graham asked again.

"Here's another, hotshot!" Woody called.

This time Graham wasn't ready at all. He was still brushing off his shirt, and his glove was tucked under his arm.

Diving to his left, he reached for the grass clipper with his *bare* hand. But Graham was unable to catch it. Still, he did somehow manage to deflect it toward Bubbles at shortstop. Since Bubbles had broken toward the hole with the crack of the bat, he backhanded the ball in his glove. In one motion, Bubbles leaped into the air, and with all the arm-strength he

**SCREAMER:**
*hard-hit fly ball.*

**PEA:**
*hard throw.*

**GRASS CLIPPER:**
*ground ball.
Also known as
"daisy cutter"
(see page 49).*

**HOLE:**
*the space between
two infielders.*

could muster, launched the pill toward first. Doc stretched for the ball, but Bubbles's throw fell short. The in-between hop tipped off Doc's glove . . . right to Tales! The Travelin' Nine's second sack man had backed up the play. He gobbled up the still-bounding ball and stomped the bag.

"Hunky play!" Doc pumped his fist.

"We still would've had him!" Tales proclaimed.

"That's what I call teamwork!" Bubbles declared.

"Every player on the infield touched the pill," Graham noted, shaking out his still-stinging hand.

Woody waved his lumber at each of his fielders before looking right at Graham. "That's what practice is all about. I reckon that's what it means to be part of a team."

**HUNKY:**
*splendid.*

**LUMBER:**
*baseball bat. Also called "timber" (see page 63).*

52

Crazy Feet pointed to the bases still out on the field.

"I'll get 'em!" Graham declared.

While the others had headed back, Graham had volunteered to help Crazy Feet gather the equipment. His mother had allowed him to stay, so long as he promised to stay close to the Travelin' Nine's left scout and do as he was told.

Graham tossed his leather to the ground and began his dash around the diamond. He ran in the reverse direction, just like Crazy Feet had during the foot race in Louisville, and scooped up each sack. When he arrived back at home dish, he dropped all four bags into the duffle Crazy Feet held open.

"That's what I call teamwork!" Graham repeated Bubbles's words from practice.

Crazy Feet nodded.

Not only was Crazy Feet a man of

**SCOUT:**
*outfielder. The right fielder was called the "right scout," the center fielder was called the "center scout," and the left fielder was called the "left scout."*

**LEATHER:**
*baseball glove or mitt.*

**53**

blazing speed, but he was also a man of deceptive strength. He picked up all three oversize duffle bags filled with the team's gear and began walking up the pathway toward Michigan Avenue where their buggy awaited.

"Would you like me to carry one?" Graham offered as he counted the number of bat heads sticking out of the ends of the bags.

Crazy Feet unhooked a finger from beneath a strap and wagged it at Graham.

"I'm stronger than you think," Graham added.

The Travelin' Nine's left scout shook his head.

"Hey, wait a second." Graham jumped into the path and held up his hand like a traffic officer. "We're missing a bat."

Graham charged off before Crazy Feet could respond, and as soon as he reached the imprint in the dirt where home dish had been, Graham spotted the lumber. It had rolled into a tuft of weeds a few yards away. He picked it up and was about to call out to Crazy Feet, when he spotted an overlooked ball in the thick patch of longer grass near where first sack used to be.

"Yes," Graham said.

He scooped up the rock and scampered to the striker's line. He peered out toward Crazy Feet, who had almost reached the avenue. Then he looked around. The only people in sight were the pedestrians on the distant street. Not a soul was watching.

"You're only getting one," Graham said, repeating Happy's refrain to him when he took his cut during the Travelin' Nine's pregame practices. He dipped his hand into his pocket and gave the baseball a good luck squeeze. "Make it count."

**ROCK:**
*baseball. Also called "pill" (see page 50) or "rawhide" (see page 132).*

**STRIKER'S LINE:**
*batter's box.*

**CUT:**
*a swing.*

55

Graham raised the bat off his shoulder, flipped the ball into the air, and swung with all his might.

*Whack!*

The ball took off like it was shot from a cannon. The cloud hunter easily cleared left garden, soared *over* Michigan Avenue, and disappeared *beyond* the tall buildings lining the far side of the busy thoroughfare. The monstrous blow left behind a faint trail of flame. Graham even thought he'd heard a distant whistle and crackle of fire as it flew.

He dropped the lumber and placed both hands on his head.

"Unbelievable," he whispered. "I don't believe what I just saw."

He couldn't wait to tell Griffith and Ruby about his mighty blast, but then he wondered if even they would believe him.

**CLOUD HUNTER:** *fly ball to the outfield, or outer garden. Also sometimes referred to as "star chaser" (see page 76) or "sky ball" (see page 148).*

**LEFT GARDEN:** *left field. The outfield was once known as the garden. So center field was referred to as "center garden" and right field was called "right garden."*

The monstrous blow left behind a faint trail of flame.

**MOON SHOT:**
*high fly ball.*

He looked about. Crazy Feet was loading the duffles onto the buggy, and he wasn't paying Graham any mind. Neither were the passersby. Nobody had seen the moon shot.

At least, so Graham thought.

# 7

★

## A Gray Day for Baseball

**riffith stood in** back of the Travelin' Nine bench, behind the rope that extended all the way down the right garden line. Since he hadn't attended practice, this was his first time at the field. He peered around at the cityscape of buildings beyond the outer garden and at the enormous lake behind him, a setting so different from where the team had played their games in Cincinnati and Louisville.

The weather was different too. From time to time, a drizzle fell, and every so often, a bank of fog rolled in off the water and blanketed the field. The gray day felt more like April than August.

Shaking the droplets of rain from his hair, Griffith turned his attention to the Chicago Nine. He had been scouting the opposing squad since they had arrived at the park, and by this point, he felt he knew the hometown ballists better than they knew themselves.

**SCOUT (v.):**
*to observe and evaluate players on the opposing side.*

What struck Griffith the most about the hometown team was the age of some of its players. Several appeared to be only a few years older than he. Their speedster shortstop with the great glove, Joe Tinker, and their second sack man, Johnny Evers, looked like some of the bigger kids in his class at school. And Ed Reulbach, their tall and skinny hurler with the live arm, couldn't have been more than sixteen or seventeen.

Leaning against the rope, Griffith looked over at his brother and sister. They needed to

be extra cautious with the ball today because they would be watching the match mere yards from the Travelin' Nine. If they weren't careful, one of the ballists could easily spot it.

But Griffith wouldn't think of watching today's contest from anywhere but right next to the barnstormers' bench. After what had happened on the train and back in Jackson Park, Griffith wanted the Travelin' Nine close by at all times.

He shook some more rain from his hair. It was going to be difficult keeping their three hands on the baseball without anyone noticing, but with the Chancellor's men nearby and closing in, what choice did they have? Griffith was certain it was only a matter of time before they made an appearance. Would they be so brazen as to try to steal the baseball from them at the game?

Peering out at the field again, Griffith

spotted Happy. Warming up down the right garden line, the Travelin' Nine's hurler seemed to be struggling to even lift his arm and kick his leg.

Griffith walked up to Doc Lindy. Even though he wasn't a real doctor (the Rough Riders had given him that nickname because of his quick thinking while helping the wounded during the war), Griffith hoped Doc could provide some insight into Happy's condition.

"I'm worried about Happy," Griffith said.

"I wouldn't be too worried," Doc replied as he arranged the players' timbers and gloves. "That old-timer always finds a way to come through."

"This is the worst he's looked."

"Let me tell you," Doc said, picking up a bat and waving it in Happy's direction, "that there is one resilient individual. For all we know, he's pulling a fast one right now.

**TIMBER:**
*baseball bat.
Also called
"lumber" (see
page 52).*

63

Making the Chicago ballists think they're going to have it easy."

Griffith exhaled. "I'm not so sure."

"My friend, never underestimate Happy. I learned that the day I met him."

"In San Antonio?"

"Oh, no, Griff." Doc leaned on the lumber. "I didn't meet these fellas in San Antonio."

"You didn't?"

"I didn't meet these men until Cuba," Doc continued. "Until San Juan Hill, as a matter of fact."

Griffith furrowed his brow. He'd always thought *all* the Travelin' Nine had met in San Antonio, Texas, where Colonel Roosevelt had assembled the Rough Riders. His father had told him countless stories of their training days; they were Griffith's favorites from the war.

"I was the Johnny-come-lately, or rather the Lindy-come-lately." Doc laughed. "But make no mistake, I'm as much a Rough Rider as anyone." He wagged the timber at Griffith. "They'll all vouch for that. Scribe, Woody, Bubbles, Crazy Feet . . ."

*"Runners!"* The umpire's call ended Doc's declaration.

"Speaking of Crazy Feet," Doc said, "let's go watch him put on a show."

In the deepest part of center garden, Crazy Feet aligned his bare toes on the timber that the umpire had placed on the turf. The Travelin' Nine's speedster was running shoeless today so as not to slip on the wet grass.

Unlike in Louisville, the race that decided which team batted first wasn't a dash around the diamond. This contest was a straight sprint across the field.

"Runners take your mark!" the umpire called.

The Chicago racer stepped forward, and

The Travelin' Nine's speedster was running shoeless today.

now the two men stood shoulder-to-shoulder at the starting line.

Ruby, Graham, and the Professor had joined Griffith and Doc, and even from half a field away, all nine eyes could see Crazy Feet's determination. He wasn't about to let what had happened back in Louisville happen again.

Behind the two runners, the flag on the flagpole just beyond center field blew harder than at any point that afternoon.

"Today's race is going to be a breeze," Graham said.

"Sounds good to me," Ruby said.

She slipped her hand into her pocket and squeezed the baseball. Then she looked at Griffith and nodded. As much as they all wanted to be holding on to their baseball for the race, they knew it wasn't possible. Not with the Professor and Doc right beside them.

**PITCHER'S HILL:**
*pitcher's mound.*

**"STRIKER TO THE LINE!":**
*what the umpire announced at the start of each contest. It was also called out at each batter's turn. Today, the umpire yells, "Batter up!"*

The umpire raised his arm above his head and shaped his fingers like a starter's pistol.

*"Go!"*

The race was never even a contest.

Like a gale-force wind, Crazy Feet blew across center garden, soared over second bag, and sailed through the infield. He even managed to dust up the damp dirt as he gusted over the pitcher's hill. He swooped into home plate, touching down on the dish with both crazy feet.

*"Striker to the line!"*

# 8

★

## The First Frame

"I t's about that time again,"
Graham said, ducking under the
rope and dragging over one of the
milk crates from beneath the players' bench.

Ruby nodded. "It sure is."

"I'll keep lookout." Graham stepped onto
the crate. "No one will see a thing."

As the Travelin' Nine took the field, Ruby
removed the baseball from her side pocket.
Like Griffith, she realized they needed to be
even more cautious than usual. She placed
her hand on Graham's back and drew him
nearer. Griffith shifted around so that when

the barnstormers returned to the bench for the bottom of the inning, they wouldn't be able to see then, either.

Griffith gazed out. As worried as he was about the Chancellor's men, he couldn't help noticing the number of people who had gathered for the midweek contest. What a crowd! The autumnlike weather hadn't affected turnout. Neither had the fact that the game was taking place in the middle of the workday. Chicagolanders loved their baseball. There were more cranks at Lake Park than at the games in Cincinnati and Louisville put together.

**CRANKS:**
*fans, usually the hometown fans. Also called "rooters" (see page 91).*

Ruby peered around also, wishfully searching the faces for Preacher Wil. He had said he might come, but so far, there had been no sign of him.

She held the baseball out to her brothers, and both boys placed their hands upon it.

"Here we go!" Graham announced.

"No one will see a thing."

The Chicago Nine's leadoff striker, their left scout who had lost to Crazy Feet in the foot race, stepped to the dish. Sensing Happy's weakened condition, he swung mightily at the first pitch, but only managed a routine grass clipper to Doc.

One hand down.

**STRIKER:**
*batter, or hitter.*

**HAND DOWN:**
*an out.* ONE HAND DOWN *meant "one out,"* TWO HANDS DOWN *meant "two outs,"* and THREE HANDS DOWN *(or* DEAD) *meant "three outs."*

That first out seemed to give Happy a shot of energy. Against the number two batter, Johnny Evers, the Chicago Nine's feisty, left-handed-hitting second sack man, Happy managed to work the plate, mixing speeds and deliveries. He threw an over-the-top pitch for strike one, dropped down and delivered a sidearm pitch for strike two, and fired his third pitch from *between his legs*.

"Strike three!" the umpire bellowed.

"Two hands down!" Griffith called.

"How 'bout Happy!" Graham cheered.

But Chicago's third batter connected, lacing Happy's pitch toward second. When Tales leaped as high as he could, the ball tipped off the top of his leather out toward right garden.

"I got it!" Woody called.

An alert gloveman, Woody had broken for the ball the moment it left the striker's bat. He nabbed the baseball on the dead run, a brilliant boot-string catch.

Three hands dead!

Woody skidded to a halt. He picked the ball from his glove, raised it over his head, and whirled around on his toes like a music-box dancer. Then he jogged *backward* toward the players' bench.

**GLOVEMAN:**
*fielder.*

**BOOT-STRING CATCH:**
*running catch made near the ground.*

"Let's go, boys!" Doc Lindy clapped as his teammates readied for their first licks. "Everyone hops on this Ferris wheel! Everyone rides around these bases."

Ruby wiped the drizzle from her cheeks and huddled her brothers in closer. Still nervous that the Travelin' Nine might notice

**BACKSTOP:**
*catcher.*

**TWO-BAGGER:**
*double.*

**GO THE
OTHER WAY:**
*when a batter hits
to the opposite side
of the field from
the one to which
he naturally hits. A
right-handed batter
going the other way
hits the ball to right
field; a left-handed
batter hits the ball
to left field.*

**HIT BEHIND
THE RUNNER:**
*when a batter hits
the ball to the right
side as a base
runner is attempting
to advance to second
or third base.*

**STINGER:**
*hard-hit ball,
usually a grounder
or a line drive.*

that they had something, she was relieved to see all the ballists focused on the field.

Crazy Feet started it off. Grabbing his favorite piece of lumber from the line of bats, he stepped to the dish. He tipped his cap to the umpire and the backstop behind the plate. Then he drove a screaming rope down the third base line. The ball hit third bag, popped into the air, and landed safely in left field. By the time the left scout retrieved the rock, Crazy Feet stood at second with a stand-up two-bagger.

Up stepped Tales. He flapped his elbow four times before each one of young Ed Reulbach's offerings. Showing patience at the line, he waited for a pitch over the outside part of the plate so that he could go the other way and hit behind the runner—which he did! He swatted a stinger down the first base line and into right field. The right scout cut the ball off, but by the time he sent it back to the infield, Crazy Feet had scored, and Tales stood safely at second.

The table setters had done it again. Back-to-back doubles. After only two strikers, the Travelin' Nine had the lead!

Now came the power portion of the barn-stormers' lineup. The next batters were all capable of reaching Michigan Avenue. Passing vehicles, bicyclists, and pedestrians needed to be alert.

Woody stepped to the dish. He pounded the plate with his timber, shuffled his feet into an ever-wider stance, and then blasted a wind-driven shot to straightaway center garden, a long round-tripper for sure.

But no!

The ball hit the billowing flag on the flag-pole beyond center garden, and it sent the pill back onto the field of play. Instead of a four-bagger, Woody had to stop at second. Yet another double—back-to-back-to-back. The Travelin' Nine now led 2 to 0.

Scribe followed with steam-power striking.

**TABLE SETTERS:** Sometimes the first two batters in the lineup are called the "table setters." They "set the table" for all the other strikers in the batting order by getting on base.

**ROUND-TRIPPER:** home run. Also called "four-bagger" (see below).

**FOUR-BAGGER:** home run. Also called "round-tripper" (see above).

He rocketed a star chaser that no flag on a flag-pole could stop.

# Home run!

"Game over!" Graham cried.

"Not so fast, Grammy," Ruby cautioned, even as the jubilant Rough Riders greeted Scribe at home dish. "We're not even out of the first frame yet."

**STAR CHASER:** *fly ball to the outfield, or outer garden. Also sometimes referred to as "cloud hunter" (see page 56) or "sky ball" (see page 148).*

"That doesn't matter." Graham raised his free fist. "The Travelin' Nine are tearing the cover off the ball!"

Griffith quickly lowered his brother's hand and anxiously looked about. More than likely, the Chancellor's men were somewhere in the vicinity, so the last thing he and his brother and sister wanted was to call attention to themselves.

With the barnstormers off to a blistering start, Professor Lance surprised everyone in the park (even his own teammates) when, instead of swinging for the city, he laid down a beauty of a bunt that stopped dead in the wet grass. An infield hit.

Doc batted next. He recorded the first out of the inning . . . on purpose. Playing team baseball, he laid down a bunt as well, a text-book sacrifice one that moved the Professor into scoring position.

Guy played team ball too. On a hit-and-run

**FRAME:**
*inning.*

**BUNT:**
*soft and short hit, often to advance a runner.*

**SACRIFICE:**
*a hit for the purpose of advancing a runner. In a sacrifice, the batter expects to record an out.*

**SCORING POSITION:**
*Any time a runner is on second or third bag, he is considered to be in scoring position.*

play, she grounded a base hit through the hole into left, past a diving Joe Tinker. The Professor easily beat the pill to the plate, and on the throw, Guy advanced to second, just as any heads-up base runner would. She then quickly moved to third on another sensational sacrifice bunt, this one by Bubbles.

Up stepped Happy with two outs and a runner on third. But Happy was barely able to swing a bat. Fortunately, he didn't have to. A rattled Reulbach had difficulty finding the strike zone, and Happy managed to work out a walk.

With runners on the corners, Crazy Feet stepped to the dish for the second time in the first frame. Guy took a walking lead off third sack, though she stood in foul territory because she remembered where Crazy Feet had smoked his leadoff double.

Smart move!

Crazy Feet lined another screamer down the left-field line. Guy trotted home, but

**HIT-AND-RUN PLAY:**
*a play in which a batter swings at the pitch while the base runner attempts to steal a base.*

**RUNNERS ON THE CORNERS:**
*When base runners occupy both first base and third base, a team is said to have runners on the corners.*

Happy was in no condition to motor around the base paths. Nevertheless, with Crazy Feet hot on his heels, Happy (like always) pushed himself too hard. Instead of stopping at third, he tried to score and was easily thrown out at the dish for the final out of the frame.

Still, what a first inning! Six runs on seven hits!

"Game over!" Graham announced again. He pumped his fist at his brother and sister and then placed it atop his other hand on the baseball. "Game over!"

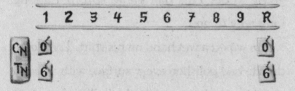

|  | 1 | 2 | 3 | 4 | 5 | 6 | 7 | 8 | 9 | R |
|---|---|---|---|---|---|---|---|---|---|---|
| CN | 0 | | | | | | | | | 0 |
| TN | 6 | | | | | | | | | 6 |

# 9

★

## A Long, Long Way to Go

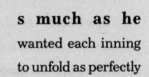

s much as he wanted each inning to unfold as perfectly as the first, Griffith realized that wasn't going to be. This ball game still had a long, long way to go.

He wiped a wet hand on his shirt. The steady drizzle had polished every surface with a coat of moisture, and as a result, the ballists from both squads struggled to run, field, and throw. And with the chilly wind blowing ever harder off Lake Michigan, it was only a matter of swings before the Chicago bats caught up to Happy's less-than-overpowering offerings and the barnstormers.

"What are you looking at?" Griffith asked Ruby, who had her back to the field and was facing the area behind home dish.

"I'm looking for Preacher Wil," she replied. "I was almost certain he would've been here by now."

"Give him time." Griffith pointed her back to the field. "It's early."

He glanced down at the baseball and then draped his shirttails over the three hands. It *was* early, Griffith thought. Plenty of time for the Chancellor's men to show. Why hadn't they yet? What were they up to?

In the top half of the second, just as Griffith had expected, the Chicago Nine fought back. Even with the three Paynes still holding on to the baseball, the Chicago Nine posted three tallies, cutting the barnstormers' lead in half.

"Happy's getting weaker by the pitch," Griffith

**TALLIES:**
*runs scored.
On some fields,
whenever the home
team scored, a
tally bell would
sound. The tally
keeper was the
official scorer,
or scorekeeper.
A tally was also
known as an "ace."*

"Happy's getting weaker by the pitch."

said as the Travelin' Nine jogged from the field.

"He's grabbing his neck and shoulder after he throws his fastballs," Ruby added.

Griffith frowned. "I know."

The Travelin' Nine managed to get one of the runs back in the bottom of the second frame when Woody launched a solo four-bagger *over* the center garden flagpole. However, in the top of the next, Chicago responded with three more runs of their own, slicing the Rough Riders' lead down to a lone tally.

**EXTRA-BASE HIT:**
*double, triple, or home run.*

In the last of the third, the barnstormers came right back again with still another solo round-tripper, this one courtesy of Guy. They would've added more than just a single run to their lead if not for the splendid glove work of Johnny Evers at second sack. He robbed Crazy Feet of an extra-base hit with a leaping grab of a rising screamer destined for the gap in right center. Then, he closed out the frame with a diving stop of Tales's grass clipper and a flip to first from his fanny.

After three innings, the Travelin' Nine led by a score of 8 to 6, but Griffith was far from at ease.

"Happy's not going to make it," he said to Ruby.

Taking his warm-up tosses prior to the start of the fourth frame, Happy struggled with his delivery. On some pitches, his foot scraped the dirt. On others, he could barely bring his arm back behind his head.

"He has to," Ruby replied. She spoke to the mist and fog and gray. "Who'll pitch if he can't?"

"That's what I'm trying to figure out."

Ruby turned to her brother. "There's six more innings to go. If he . . ."

Out of the corner of her eye, she spotted the

| | 1 | 2 | 3 | 4 | 5 | 6 | 7 | 8 | 9 | R |
|---|---|---|---|---|---|---|---|---|---|---|
| CN | 0 | 3 | 3 | | | | | | | 6 |
| TN | 6 | 1 | 1 | | | | | | | 8 |

# 10

★

## *The Eagle and the Breeze*

e's here!" **Ruby** said, pointing.

"Who is?" Graham asked.

"Preacher Wil," Ruby replied, slipping the baseball safely back into her pocket for the time being. "He said he'd show up, and he did!"

"Who's Preacher Wil?" Graham pressed.

"We met him in the park," Griffith answered.

Griffith saw him now too. He stood behind the cranks who were watching the match down the third base line.

"Which one is he?" Graham asked, standing on his toes atop the crate.

"The tall, dark one," Ruby answered. "The one with the smile."

In the distance, Preacher Wil slowly raised his hand, the one with the missing finger, and waved.

"Now I see him!" Graham exclaimed.

Ruby glanced to Griffith. "Let's go say hello."

"Not a chance," Griffith replied instantly. "We're not going anywhere. And don't even think about going by yourself."

"I wasn't going to." Ruby folded her arms tightly across her chest and glared at her older brother.

Griffith made a face. "If you say so."

Ruby turned from Griffith and peered back out at the field. The fourth frame was yet to begin. On the hill, all of the Travelin' Nine infielders had gathered around Happy.

Even the umpire had joined the meeting on the mound. Everyone wanted to know if the hurler was healthy enough to pitch. (He was insisting he was.)

"You know I'm right," Griffith whispered in Ruby's ear. "It's not safe."

Ruby traced a thumb back and forth over her bottom lip. Of course, she knew he was right. Like Griffith, she knew the Chancellor's men had to be out there. Lurking. Still, Ruby wondered about Preacher Wil. What if—

"Where'd he go?" Graham suddenly asked.

Ruby whirled around. Preacher Wil was no longer there.

"He was there a second ago," Graham added.

Griffith stood on his toes and searched the crowd.

Ruby wiped the drizzle from her face. "How could he just disappear like that?"

"It's not safe."

"Let's use those," Graham said, pointing beneath the Travelin' Nine bench. He ducked under the rope, quickly retrieved two more milk crates, and slipped back next to his siblings.

"Good idea," Ruby said, as her little brother stacked the crates and climbed on. She hopped up beside him.

However, Griffith wasn't so sure it was a good idea. In a way, it was almost as if his brother and sister were inviting the Chancellor's goons to come find them. Then again, if the crates raised them high enough to attract attention, the thugs may have already spotted them. Griffith reasoned that his climbing up wasn't likely to make a difference and he also might be able to detect the Chancellor's men. So he joined Ruby and Graham.

"I can see the entire park," Ruby said.

"I can see all of Chicago," Griffith added.

"I can see over everyone!" Graham exclaimed. "I can't wait to be this tall!"

"Keep on waiting, *little* brother," Griffith said with a smirk. "First, you have to be taller than me, and that's not happening any time soon."

All three searched the park, but there was no sign of Preacher Wil anywhere.

"Speaking of soon," Ruby said after a few moments, "we need for *things* to start happening." On the field, the ballists and umpire were returning to their positions. At long last, the inning was getting set to begin. She dipped her hand into her side pocket. "I say it's about time they did."

"I don't know if we should take it out up here," Griffith said. His eyes remained glued to the rooters, but he saw no sign of the Chancellor's crew.

Ruby motioned to the cranks. "The match is starting up again. Everyone's looking at

**ROOTERS:** *fans; people who cheer at ball games. Also called "cranks" (see page 70).*

the field. No one's paying attention to us."

"The Travelin' Nine are winning," Griffith answered. "I'm not sure if we need to use the ball."

"Let's see if anything happens," Ruby said, tilting her head. "We'll keep it under your shirt again. Come on, Griff. We can at least try."

Griffith sighed. "Fine."

Ruby lifted out the baseball and quickly hid it under Griffith's shirt. Both boys slipped their hands beneath the tails. The moment all three hands joined together on the ball, *it* appeared.

It started as a tiny speck beyond the barrier of buildings. Slowly, it took shape as it soared in from over the Chicago skyscrapers, growing larger during its glide and descent toward the field. Faster and faster it approached, its broad wings making a deep blowing sound like the exhaust from a hot air balloon. Then suddenly it swooped down over the crowd, lifting the hats off the gentlemen and blowing the bonnets from the ladies.

"A bald eagle!" Graham exclaimed.

"I haven't seen one of those since back home," Ruby said.

"I have," Griffith whispered.

"You have?" Ruby and Graham asked at the same time.

Griffith nodded. "I've seen *that* bald eagle."

"Where?" Graham asked.

"On the *Meriwether*. On the way to Louisville."

"Why didn't you tell us?" Ruby asked.

But Griffith was too entranced by the bird to answer.

As it had on the steamer, the sight of the eagle stirred up the memory of that day many years ago. Clearer than ever, Griffith could see the enormous bird snatching Graham from his wicker bassinet and carrying him

Then suddenly it swooped down over the crowd . . .

off. He could hear his mother's wails as she cried on the family room sofa. And he could see his father, Uncle Owen, and all their neighbors frantically racing up and down the streets in search of his brother.

But now, he remembered something *new*. It was as if a portal to a corner of his brain had been opened, and within was a long-forgotten memory, hidden because of the pain and anguish surrounding it.

The man with the different-colored eyes had been there. Griffith could see him standing on the other side of the screen door on their front porch, looking just as bedraggled as he had in the park. His beard was long and gray, his clothing old and weathered. And he was holding the baseball.

That's when the ball had *arrived*. The baseball hadn't been there prior to Graham's being carried off. It had appeared only after his safe return and never moved from the stand beside Graham's bed until their father left for the war.

Griffith looked to his little brother. "Does that eagle look familiar to you?" he asked.

"Should it?"

Griffith paused. "Maybe. Maybe not."

"Thanks for clearing that up." Graham rolled his eyes.

Griffith watched the bird fade into the gray Chicago sky. Why had the eagle returned? What did the eagle have to do with the baseball? And what did the man with the unusual eyes have to do with any of it?

When the eagle had completely vanished, the steady mist and drizzle stopped, and the patches of fog hovering above the outer garden disappeared.

Then came the gust. A hot breeze. Like the blast from an opening furnace. As if the breeze were made of fire. On an afternoon almost cool enough for cranks and ballists and kids to be able to see their breath, a blazing gale blew through. Everyone felt the wind, and if anything could stir fear into the hearts and minds of Chicagolanders, it was the mere thought of fire in the air.

"I think we did that," Griffith said.

"No doubt about it," Ruby added. "We absolutely did that."

"How do you know for sure?" Griffith asked.

Ruby lifted the baseball out from under

Griffith's shirt and pointed to the stream of smoke rising from the acorn-size hole. And within that hole, the embedded object glowed orange and yellow.

"It's also hot," Ruby said, shaking it. "Our baseball is hot."

| | 1 | 2 | 3 | 4 | 5 | 6 | 7 | 8 | 9 | R |
|---|---|---|---|---|---|---|---|---|---|---|
| CN | 0 | 3 | 3 | | | | | | | 6 |
| TN | 6 | 1 | 1 | | | | | | | 8 |

# 11

★

## *Fireballs*

**appy needs to be a** fireballer," Graham said to Ruby, unstacking the milk crates and tossing the extra ones to the side. "That's what Daddy called hurlers who threw hard."

"Fireballers and flame-throwers," Ruby added. She cradled the warm baseball in her hands as Happy sized up the leadoff striker.

Graham glanced at his brother. "That has to be it, right, Griffy?" he asked, stepping back onto the crate he had perched upon earlier. He left space for his sister, who joined him. "We're in Chicago. It's all about fire and flames."

Griffith had shared with Graham what he had learned about Chicago from Happy. Graham had been riveted when he'd told him about the Great Fire.

However, Griffith didn't answer his younger brother. As he slide-stepped to his left and positioned himself between the bench and his siblings, his concern over Ruby and Graham standing on even the single crate grew. Griffith could see it provided them with a clearer view of the action on the field, but they stood out. People were able to see their faces.

The Chancellor's men were up to something. With each passing moment, Griffith was more sure of it. The encounter on the train had been merely a prelude. But what did they have in store for him and his brother and sister? Why was there still no sign of them? Why . . .

Griffith whirled around. He was certain there would be someone there. And for a fleeting instant, he thought he'd spotted the familiar handkerchief in the suit pocket of a man only a few persons away. But no. What he'd seen was a girl huddled next to her father, her pink hair ribbon pressed to his suit jacket.

Turning back toward the match, Griffith eased closer to Ruby and Graham. He would try to focus solely on the game. Even though the Travelin' Nine were already ahead, the eagle and the wind told him *things* were about to happen. He reached over, joining his hand to his siblings' on the still-warm sphere.

"Bring the heat!" Ruby cheered.

"You're a fireballer, Happy!" Graham shouted.

"Fastballs, Happy!" Griffith chimed in, cupping his free hand over his mouth. "Only fastballs!"

On the hill, Happy tipped his cap to the three Paynes and then stepped to the pitcher's line. It was time for hot stuff and nothing else. No more side-arm pitches, behind-the-back offerings, or between-the-legs deliveries.

Happy reached into his glove, stared down the striker, rocked into his windup, and fired his first pitch.

Fire he did! A trail of flame streaked behind the ball.

"Strike one!" the umpire called.

As soon as the Travelin' Nine hurler saw the flames, he shook out his thumb and three fingers, but they weren't even warm. With a puzzled expression, he stared at his digits.

For his second pitch, Happy followed instructions and fired another heater. Once again, a ball of flame left his grip and blazed a path across the plate.

"Strike two!"

A trail of flame streaked behind the ball.

Happy couldn't help shaking out his fingers and hand again, but they still were as cool as the damp air around him.

After his third pitch—another fastball and another strike—Happy didn't bother to shake out his fingers and hand. By then, he knew there was no need.

"Yer out!" the umpire sang.

"Smokin'!" Graham declared.

"Did you see those pitches?" Ruby asked.

"I sure did." Griffith patted his chest and then pointed to the striker returning to his bench. "But he didn't!"

"He can't see the fireballs?" Graham asked.

"No way," Griffith replied. "If that striker had seen great balls of fire coming at him, he wouldn't have stood at the line. He'd have run for the hills!"

While the next batter made his way to the dish, Ruby glanced around. She searched the cranks standing behind the home squad's bench and those watching the match from down the right garden line. Preacher Wil still hadn't reappeared.

The next two Chicago Nine strikers were also overmatched. With each one of Happy's offerings, they turned away, bailed out, or jumped back—not because they saw the balls aflame, but because the balls flew in so fast, they could barely see them blowing by! On one pitch, the first striker hopped half-way back to his bench, and on another, the second striker dove to the ground, ending up with a face full of mud.

Happy struck out the side on only ten pitches. He would've struck out the side on nine . . . but the umpire missed a call when *he* ducked away from a blazing fastball.

| | 1 | 2 | 3 | 4 | 5 | 6 | 7 | 8 | 9 | R |
|----|---|---|---|---|---|---|---|---|---|---|
| CN | 0 | 3 | 3 | 0 | | | | | | 6 |
| TN | 6 | 1 | 1 | | | | | | | 8 |

# 12

★

## *Bats on Fire*

ou're the bosses," Tales said as the Travelin' Nine returned to the bench for the last half of the fourth frame.

"We're all ears," Bubbles added, scratching what remained of his partially missing left ear. "Well, I'm *almost* all ears."

As soon as Ruby had seen the players coming their way, she had lifted her brothers' hands from the ball and tucked it away. When the ballists neared, she and Graham had hopped off the crate.

Then, like she so often did, Ruby dipped

her hand into her pocket and rested it on the baseball. She thought back to the moment Uncle Owen gave them the ball. *No one can know of this.* She heard his words in her head. She knew they needed to keep the ball secret. So much was at stake, and it was so important for the Rough Riders to win.

"Only swing at fastballs," Griffith instructed.

"That's right," Graham added. He stood in the center of the huddle and pretended to be a hurler. "Wait for the heat!"

"How am I to know when he's bringin' the flames?" Woody asked. The barnstormers' right scout was leading off the frame.

"Oh, you'll know," Ruby said, smiling confidently. With a fingernail, she teased the baseball's hot stitching.

"Don't worry about a thing," Griffith added.

Ruby pulled her hand from her pocket and blew on her fingers.

"You cold?" Woody asked.

"Not exactly."

Woody set himself at the striker's line. He took the first pitch, a changeup out of the strike zone.

**CHANGEUP:**
*slow pitch thrown with the exact same arm action as a fastball, designed to disrupt the timing of the hitter.*

"Ball!" the umpire barked.

Woody peeked over at Ruby, and she nodded back. She had asked him to show patience at the dish while she and her brothers searched for signs and figured out what he should do.

The hurler delivered his next pitch, another changeup off the plate.

"Ball!" the umpire barked again.

Griffith stroked his chin. Young Eddie Reulbach had a live arm on the hill, but he had only two pitches in his arsenal, a fastball and a changeup. He had tremendous raw talent (just like Graham), but he was still learning what it meant to be an accomplished hurler. Behind in the count, the next pitch would certainly be a fastball.

"Get ready, Woody," Griffith said through gritted teeth.

Reulbach rocked into his windup. As soon as he released the pitch, sparks and then flames shot from the end of Woody's lumber. A startled Woody dropped the timber as the pill crossed the plate.

"Strike!" the umpire cried.

Woody didn't react. He simply stared at his *smoldering* bat lying in the dirt at his feet.

"Pick it up!" Graham shouted.

"I reckon it's too hot!" Woody shouted back.

"No, it's not," Graham replied. "You won't get burned!"

"You ain't supposed to play with fire," Woody argued.

"Striker!" the umpire interjected. "Pick up your timber and prepare to hit."

Griffith, Ruby, and Graham all looked at one another. At the same instant, they realized the umpire hadn't seen the sparks and flames. Nor could he see the smoke still rising from the barrel of the bat.

Graham clenched both fists and pumped them in Woody's direction. "You trust us, right?" he called.

With that, Woody reached down and

picked up his bat, and from the way he gripped the wood, all three Paynes knew they were right. The timber wasn't even hot. Woody tightened his grasp and dug in for the next pitch.

As soon as the pitch left Reulbach's hand, once again, the tip of Woody's timber started to flicker. By the time the ball reached the plate, the entire end of the bat had burst into flames.

**ALLEY:**
*either of two areas in the outfield, one between left garden and center garden and the other between right garden and center garden.*

But this time around, Woody held on. He swung mightily and blasted the rock to the outer garden. Erupting from the batter's box, Woody tore around the bases as his drive split the alley between center and right. He didn't stop running until he was all the way at third.

"Woody!" Graham cheered. "Woody!"

Using an array of scorching line drives, searing grass clippers, and smoking cloud hunters,

The entire end of the bat had burst into flames.

the Travelin' Nine piled on four more runs. At the end of the frame, they had doubled up the Chicago Nine and led by a score of 12 to 6.

The Chicago Nine and their cranks knew that the Travelin' Nine's bats were *hot*, but they couldn't see the flames on them any more than they could see Happy's fireballs—which was a good thing since the smoke and fire certainly would've terrified the locals.

Still, even with the widening lead, Griffith had reason to worry. On the hill, Happy had been setting aside the Chicago strikers one after another, but he was showing the strain of throwing so many fastballs. He would grunt on some pitches and groan after others. And his shoulders slumped lower and lower with each recorded out.

Who would pitch when Happy no longer could? Griffith needed to be thinking ahead. A good manager—a team leader—was always looking forward, planning the next strategic move. That's how his father had played the game of baseball. On the green oasis, his father had always seemed to be one step ahead of everyone else.

GREEN OASIS: *playing field. Also called the "pitch" (see page 137).*

That was Griffith's job now.

| | 1 | 2 | 3 | 4 | 5 | 6 | 7 | 8 | 9 | R |
|---|---|---|---|---|---|---|---|---|---|---|
| CN | 0 | 3 | 3 | 0 | | | | | | 6 |
| TN | 6 | 1 | 1 | 4 | | | | | | 12 |

# 13

★

## The Number Thirty-one

**PLATE (v.):**
*to score a run,
or tally.*

**n the fifth frame, the** Travelin' Nine poured it on, adding to the four runs they plated in the fourth. However, for this rally, the barnstormers didn't swat the ball all over the green oasis. Instead, they relied on their base-running prowess.

On the hill, Young Eddie Reulbach

changed tactics. No longer did he throw strictly fastballs and changeups. He fired palm balls and screwballs, confusing the Travelin' Nine strikers. But his new approach came with a price. He issued seven bases on balls.

The Rough Riders lit up the base paths in the fifth frame. Frequently when one of the ballists reached base (which was quite often), a lane of fire ignited to the next sack. It took Ruby all of one base runner to realize the locals couldn't see this fire either. And that was also how long it took her to figure out the paths of fire were signaling for the barnstormers to steal. Running on fire, each member of the Travelin' Nine flew almost as

**PALM BALL:**
pitch thrown by holding the ball tightly between the palm and thumb.

**SCREWBALL:**
pitch that breaks or curves from left to right.

**BASE ON BALLS:**
a walk. If a batter receives four pitches out of the strike zone in one plate appearance, he advances to first base.

fast as Crazy Feet. Both Bubbles and Tales stole two bases apiece, but it was Woody who executed the most daring theft of all. Perfectly timing Eddie Reulbach's pitch to the plate, Woody stole home, sneaking his boot under the tag of the stunned catcher's mitt. All told, the Rough Riders swiped eight bases and scored five runs in the inning.

Happy continued to fade in the top of the sixth, but he still somehow managed to set aside the hometown ballists in order. Griffith had no idea where the old-timer was finding his strength and stamina.

**BATTED AROUND:** *when all nine players on a team take a turn at the plate during a single inning.*

In the bottom of the frame, the barn-stormers' bats were back in business. Abandoning his wild pitches, the hometown hurler returned to throwing fastballs and changeups, and once again, the Travelin' Nine's lumber caught fire. The Rough Riders batted around and walloped the rock all over the field. By the end of the inning, the barnstormers had tacked on six more tallies, and heading to the seventh, they led by the whopping margin of 23 to 6.

But in spite of the score and the raw and rainy weather, the cranks remained. Chicagolanders did indeed love their baseball, and they were witnessing a highly skilled brand of it, courtesy of the Travelin' Nine.

"Game over!" Graham declared yet again. "We're in the money!"

Griffith responded as he had before. "Not so fast, Grammy."

"What do you mean 'not so fast'? We're winning twenty-three to six. Do the math. Twenty-three, Griff!"

"Little brother, from what I've learned, they're used to high-scoring affairs in the Windy City. In this town, when a team scores twenty-three runs, the next question people ask is 'Who's winning?'"

Graham patted his chest. "Well, I'm not asking."

Griffith shook his head. The Travelin' Nine may have been ahead by seventeen runs, but a reality was setting in.

Happy had just about run out of gas. With the last strikers he had faced in the sixth, Happy'd had to stop a few times in the middle of the windup and start again. And he had been unable to muster enough strength to rock into his delivery, to boot.

**RETIRED THE SIDE:** *when the pitcher or defensive team has recorded the three outs in an inning.*

"Happy's done," Griffith said to Ruby, as the Travelin' Nine's hurler took the hill.

"What do you mean 'he's done'?" She eyed him sideways. "He's pitching great. He retired the side on ten pitches in the fourth, eleven pitches in the fifth, and ten again in the sixth. How can he be done?"

"Trust me. That's about to change. He's done."

Ruby tucked her wet hair behind her ears.

"Sorry. A pitcher doesn't just lose it after setting down nine straight on only thirty-one pitches."

Griffith's eyes popped. "What did you just say?"

"What?"

"That last thing. About thirty-one pitches. Say it again."

"Allow me," Graham answered first. He pretended to tuck his hair behind his ears like Ruby had a moment ago. "A pitcher doesn't just lose it after setting down nine straight on only thirty-one pitches."

"That's how I know!" Griffith placed a hand on each of their shoulders. "Check this out: The Chicago Fire lasted for *thirty-one* hours. Happy taught me that. After *thirty-one* pitches, Happy's fire is out too."

Ruby shook her head. "He's thrown far more than thirty-one pitches, Griff."

Griffith thought for a moment, then

snapped his fingers. "That's how many pitches he's thrown since we saw the eagle and felt the wind."

"But if Happy can't pitch, who will?" Ruby asked.

"I'll pitch!" Graham offered. He wound up like he had earlier. "You know I could."

"You can't pitch in this game," Griffith said flatly.

But Graham wasn't about to let his brother's response be the final word. He hopped off the crate, ducked under the rope, and stepped as close as he could get to his mother at backstop without setting foot on the field.

"Guy," Graham called, "can I ask you a question?"

"What is it?" she asked, lifting her mask and adjusting her cap so that none of her long hair slipped out.

"If the Travelin' Nine ever need a ballist, like a substitute, could I be that ballist?"

Her look answered his question.

"I told you," Griffith said. He had followed after Graham and now took him by the arm. "Come on. We can't leave Ruby by herself."

Just as Griffith had predicted, Happy began to falter. His fastballs no longer turned to fireballs, and the Chicago Nine strikers pounced.

Leading off the seventh, Joe Tinker laced a screamer into left garden for a base hit. Johnny Evers followed with a two-bagger to the gap between center and right garden.

**TEXAS LEAGUER:** *bloop hit that drops between infielder and outfielder.*

Base hit. Triple. Base hit. Base hit.

In almost no time, four runs had crossed the plate. Only some stellar glove work by Bubbles, which included a sliding-splashing catch of a Texas leaguer in short left garden to close out the frame, prevented further damage.

On the walk back to the bench after the last out, Happy had to stop and rest twice.

Griffith climbed over the rope and sat down beside him. "How are you feeling?" he asked, placing his hand on Happy's leg.

"I've felt better."

Happy's words sent a chill through Griffith. He had never heard Happy complain about anything or admit that something was wrong.

"One of the other Rough Riders can pitch," Griffith said.

Happy wiped his brow with his forearm. "Think I got one more in me," he said to his boots resting in a puddle.

Griffith let out a long breath. If Happy could pitch one more inning—and that seemed like a mighty big if—it still left the ninth inning. Who was going to relieve Happy? Perhaps Woody, with his cannon-like arm. Or maybe Doc Lindy, who threw harder than all the other infielders. The professor was a crafty ballist: Surely he'd find a

"How are you feeling?"

way to retire three strikers. Griffith stroked his chin. Certainly not Bubbles, Crazy Feet, or Scribe. The Travelin' Nine needed their steady gloves in the field. And definitely not Tales. He could make the toss from second bag to first better than anyone, but that was the only throw he could make. Maybe Guy could pitch. But then who would catch?

Griffith gazed around at the seventh-inning stretch festivities. A four-piece band circled the diamond. Jugglers and clowns performed along the foul lines. Some of the vendors sold beverages, while the others tossed free boxes of Cracker Jacks and packets of Wrigley's gum to the cranks—just like they had advertised.

However, Griffith didn't want any part of the fun. As he looked from lake to sky to city, the only thing he wanted was to make sure the Travelin' Nine hung on and won. A victory today—with such a large crowd on hand—would net hundreds of dollars, money the Paynes desperately needed to pay off their enormous debt. Griffith's single-minded determination even managed to push aside thoughts of the Chancellor and his men.

But only momentarily. The Chancellor's men were out there. Without a doubt. They were plotting, scheming. Griffith couldn't let his guard down.

"Don't fret, Griff." Happy reached over and patted Griffith's leg. "The Rough Riders will find the way. We always do."

| | 1 | 2 | 3 | 4 | 5 | 6 | 7 | 8 | 9 | R |
|---|---|---|---|---|---|---|---|---|---|---|
| C_N | 0 | 3 | 3 | 0 | 0 | 0 | 4 | | | 10 |
| T_N | 6 | 1 | 1 | 4 | 5 | 6 | | | | 23 |

# 14

★

*Sounds from Beyond*

n the bottom of the sev-
enth, the Travelin' Nine couldn't
even manage a foul tick. Tales
struck out on three straight pitches, swinging wildly at offerings way out of the strike
zone. Woody fanned as well—the last pitch
he swung at bounced halfway between home
plate and the hurler's hill. As for Scribe, his
timber never left his shoulder.

Everyone was far too distracted by the
sound.

"What is that?" Graham asked.

"I have no idea," Griffith replied.

**FOUL TICK:**
*foul ball that
barely touches the
hitter's bat.*

**FAN (v.):**
*to strike out.*

"I can't even tell where it's coming from," Ruby added.

She spun around. One minute, she was certain the earth-shaking groan was originating from the buildings across Michigan Avenue. But the next moment, she was equally sure the two-toned, foghornlike bellow was coming from the clouds above Lake Michigan. And as she looked about, Ruby realized the locals weren't paying any mind to the rumblings underfoot or to what sounded like a distant tuba repeating the same off-key notes.

For now, all she could do was hope that the strange noise would have the same effect on the Chicago Nine strikers as it did on the barnstormers.

Joe Tinker, the leadoff batter for the Chicago Nine in the top half of the eighth frame, swung at Happy's first pitch.

*Boom!*

Out in right garden, Woody didn't flinch. His hands never left his knees. As the rawhide soared by, he didn't even bother to turn around. He simply shook his head once. There was no doubt about that moon shot. It was destined to travel halfway across Cook County.

Chicago's next batter didn't bother swinging because none of Happy's pitches was anywhere close. Happy issued a four-pitch base on balls.

**RAWHIDE:** *baseball. Also called "pill" (see page 50) or "rock" (see page 55).*

Up stepped the third striker. Following Joe Tinker's approach, he jumped all over Happy's first offering (even though it was out of the strike zone).

*Boom!*

Like Woody in right garden two hitters before, Crazy Feet out in left didn't move a muscle as the rock sailed past. He simply lowered his head. From the moment the ball left the bat, there was no doubt the torpedoed drive was heading for the Chicago city limits.

Happy had faced three batters and given up three runs.

Ruby looked down at their three hands atop the baseball. It wasn't making a difference. Her pinky was even inside the acorn-size hole, but Happy was still melting down.

"That's it," she suddenly said. "I can't just stand here and not do anything."

"What are you going to do?" Griffith asked.

Ruby exhaled a frustrated puff and gazed out at the city. The sound was coming from out there. That much she was sure of. With each hit and run, the echo off the buildings had grown louder. It—whatever *it* was—was getting closer, too.

"What am I going to do?" she replied. "What you did."

"No, Ruby. You're not. They might see you."

"If they're here, Griff, they've already

seen us." She passed the baseball to her older brother. "How could they not?"

Griffith shook his head. "It's asking for trouble. They could . . ."

"What are you two talking about?" Graham interrupted. "Who's they?"

"Um, er, they," Griffith answered, turning to his younger brother. "People at . . . people at the park," he stammered. "The people who keep everyone but the ballists off the field."

"Too late!" Graham pointed.

Just like Griffith back in Louisville, Ruby had charged onto the field.

"Time out!" she called.

"Time!" the umpire shouted, leaping out from behind the plate. "Young'un, leave the field!"

But Ruby ignored the order. She waved the rest of the infielders to the mound.

"Who can pitch?" she asked right away, taking the ball from Happy.

"Who can pitch?"

Silence.

Out of the corner of her eye, she could see the umpire was only steps away. She turned to Professor Lance. With Happy dragging, he had assumed the leadership role among the Travelin' Nine infielders. He had become the one who reminded the others of the number of outs, where to make the throws, and where to stand for different strikers.

But right now, the Professor glared. "You don't belong out here, Ruby," he said.

"I'm only trying to help," she answered.

"We all understand that, but this intrusion disrespects the game."

Ruby frowned. "I didn't mean to. I just wanted to find out who else could pitch."

"I vote for Scribe," Tales blurted.

"I second it." Bubbles raised his hand.

"Third," Doc said. "His size alone will intimidate the strikers. Crazy Feet and Woody can close the gaps in the outer garden, and—"

"Enough!" the umpire interrupted. "Everyone back to their positions." He grabbed the ball and returned it to Happy. "You're still pitching." Then he spun to Ruby.

"Now, you listen to me, young lady."

"Yes, sir," Ruby replied softly.

The umpire pointed down at her. "In Chicagoland, they like to say 'Beware the cow that kicks.' But I have news for you. This umpire kicks harder than any cow. Now get off *my* field before I have you escorted from this park."

Ruby didn't need to be told again. She scampered off the pitch and back to Griffith and Graham.

**PITCH:**
*playing field.*
*Also called*
*"green oasis"*
*(see page 117).*

"Beware the cow that kicks," she said when she reached her brothers.

As soon as Ruby uttered those five words . . .

| | 1 | 2 | 3 | 4 | 5 | 6 | 7 | 8 | 9 | R |
|------|---|---|---|---|---|---|---|---|---|----|
| CN | 0 | 3 | 3 | 0 | 0 | 0 | 4 | 3 | | 13 |
| TM | 6 | 1 | 1 | 4 | 5 | 6 | | | | 23 |

# 15

★

## *Holy Cow!*

t emerged from between the brick buildings, head and shoulders towering above the offices, hotels, and apartment complexes. It was the size of several hot air balloons— but heavy. As it stepped forth from the city streets, the ground shook with each of its deliberate movements. When it reached Michigan Avenue, not a single vehicle on the bustling thoroughfare slowed, swerved, or stopped.

"Holy cow!" Graham exclaimed, his forearm in front of his face.

Griffith shielded his eyes. "What made you say that?" he asked Ruby.

"'Beware the cow that kicks'?" she replied. "That's what the umpire said to me."

"That's what Happy told me in Jackson Park."

Down on the field, as the next hometown striker stepped to the line, the cranks continued to clap and whistle and hoot, cheering on the improbable comeback. No, none of the locals could see or feel it.

**STEP TO THE LINE (v.):** *to prepare to hit.*

But the Travelin' Nine could, and when that first house-size hoof landed in center garden, the ballists scrambled. Crazy Feet broke for the left garden line, Woody bolted toward the right garden line, and Scribe fled to the infield. Until now, none of the oddities on the field during any of the matches had frightened the Rough Riders. But the colossal cow terrified them.

Of course, the umpire was also oblivious

to the animal's arrival, so when the Travelin' Nine interrupted the action yet again, he showed little patience.

"Play ball!" he ordered. "Return to your positions, or I will declare this game a forfeit."

Even the cranks grew restless. To them, it appeared as if the Travelin' Nine were exhibiting bad sportsmanship and delaying the game on purpose. Some began to boo. Some hurled insults.

As for Griffith, Ruby, and Graham, they realized they didn't have to be frightened, but they still collectively cowered atop the milk crate. All three held on to their ball *and* one another.

Griffith huddled his sister and brother in close. However, he was no longer staring at the cow, he was searching the crowd. Everyone in the park had seen Ruby run on and off the field. If the Chancellor's men were here, they now knew exactly where

The colossal cow terrified them.

they were standing. The thugs could be working their way through the crowd and toward them at this moment.

His chest tightened. Griffith wanted to scold Ruby. By running onto the green oasis, she had put all three of them in danger. But what good would berating her do? It would only make her feel bad, and that wouldn't accomplish anything.

"What on earth is a cow doing here?" Graham asked.

"Better yet, what is a gargantuan cow doing here?" Ruby asked.

"I think I know this cow," Griffith answered.

Ruby eyed him sideways (though from where she stood, it was rather difficult to eye him any other way). "You do?"

"What is it with you and animals these days?" Graham asked. "First you knew the eagle, and now you know the gigantic cow."

Griffith nodded once. "I think that may be Mrs. O'Leary's cow."

"Mrs. who?" Graham asked.

"Mrs. O'Leary," Griffith replied. "Her cow kicked over the lantern that started the Great Fire."

"That's not how it really began," Ruby said, shaking her head. "From what I heard, that's a tall tale."

"And that's one tall cow," Griffith said with a smile.

"Well, if you ask me," Graham said, "I don't care who that cow is, or what fire it did or didn't start. I only want to know what it's going to do now!"

For the moment, it just stood there, flicking its ears and sniffing the air. It no longer mooed, but it took up all of center garden and Scribe's place on the green oasis.

So Scribe took over at a new position: hurler. Yes, the Travelin' Nine used the opportunity to switch hurlers, and since the umpire was demanding that the game resume, he no longer protested the pitching change.

"I hope they don't hit it to center," Graham said.

"You and me both, Grammy." Ruby squeezed her brother's hand on the baseball.

Griffith looked out at Happy, the team's new center scout, who stood in front of second sack. "That makes three of us."

The Chicago Nine did hit to center garden. And they sprayed hits to left and right, too. The first three hometown strikers that Scribe faced all reached base safely.

"He shouldn't be pitching," Ruby said to her brothers.

"His fastballs aren't fireballs," Graham added.

"Exactly," Griffith said. "That's why I don't think he's the right hurler either."

As imposing as Scribe may have seemed standing atop the mound, his intimidating presence was having no effect on the home-town hitters. The Chicago Nine picked up where they had left off against Happy, piling on the hits and runs.

Base hit. Triple. Base hit. Base hit. Triple.

Of course, the hits to center garden sent the cranks into a frenzy. Since the locals couldn't see the on-field obstacle, it appeared to them as though the baseball was doing the impossible—making right turns in midair, reversing course, and smacking into invis-ible walls. They roared and laughed while watching Woody, Crazy Feet, and Bubbles pursue the elusive pill.

The Travelin' Nine, on the other hand, were hardly amused or entertained. When one sky ball hit the cow on the nose (causing the pill to take a hard right), Woody had to chase after the redirected rock with the angry bovine breathing heavily behind his back. Another frozen rope clanked the cowbell dangling from the bovine's neck (or to the locals, bounded off a nonexistent barrier).

"That's a good cow," Bubbles said as he tiptoed between the huge hooves and through a puddle of cow drool to retrieve the rawhide. "Easy, girl," he whispered, staring into the flaring nostrils.

With five more hits and four more runs, the once seemingly insurmountable lead was down to a score of 23 to 17.

But then Scribe settled in against the next two hitters. He retired the first one on a comebacker, holding the runner at third. He disposed of the next on a pop to the Professor. It appeared as though he was pitching out of the jam.

**SKY BALL:** *fly ball to the outfield, or outer garden. Also sometimes referred to as "cloud hunter" (see page 56) or "star chaser" (see page 76).*

**COMEBACKER:** *ground ball hit directly to the pitcher.*

"That's a good cow. . . . Easy, girl."

Not so fast.

Scribe walked the next two strikers, and all of a sudden, the bases were loaded again. With one whip of the willow, the Chicago Nine could be back to within two.

"That's it!" Ruby announced again. She leaped off the crate and turned to her brothers. "We can't just stand here and do nothing."

**WHIP OF THE WILLOW:** *swing of the bat.*

"You're not planning on running onto the field again, are you?" Griffith asked.

"You'll get thrown out of the park," Graham added.

"We need to do what we did in Louisville," Ruby said, cupping the baseball with both hands and holding it to her chest.

"We are," Graham said.

"No, we're not," Ruby shot back. "Yes, we're watching the game and holding the baseball, but we're fearing the worst. The Travelin' Nine need us behind them. We

150

need to believe in them, not doubt them."

Griffith nodded. What Ruby was saying was correct. But ever since Ruby had run onto the field, he hadn't been able to stop thinking about the Chancellor and his men. Where were they? With each passing moment, their absence grew more and more unsettling.

He blinked hard and then looked to his sister. "You're right, Ruby," Griffith said. "We all need to hold on to the baseball with only encouraging thoughts in our heads."

"We can't wait any longer," Ruby said, stepping back onto the crate and motioning for her brothers to join her. "And I hope we haven't waited too long." She looked from Griffith to Graham. "They need one out. Let's help them get it."

The three siblings huddled together and joined hands on the baseball. Ruby inserted her pinky into the odd, acorn-size hole.

In the outer garden, Crazy Feet and Woody had returned to their regular positions. As unnerved as they may have been by the monstrous bovine, both ballists realized how much was riding on this batter.

When Scribe raised his arms, the three runners led off each base. Then as he rotated into his motion, every runner took off. A triple steal!

All three hands holding the baseball shot forward, pointing toward the third base line, where the runner had broken for the dish.

Scribe threw his pitch. The Chicago striker swung.

*Crack!*

A towering fly ball. Deep down the left garden line.

All three hands—already extended in the general direction of the action—followed the flight of the ball. Since everyone was looking at the field, no one paid any mind to the three Paynes.

Suddenly, the center garden cow began whipping her tail, and as soon as she did, all three outstretched arms *shifted*. No longer did they trace the track of the rocketed blast; instead, they pointed at the bovine's behind.

Three startled Paynes glanced at one another.

"Crazy Feet!" they shouted together.

The Travelin' Nine's left scout, who had been charging toward the left field line after the cloud hunter, heard the call. Spotting the pointing Paynes out of the corner of his eye, he swerved and started to run full speed *away* from the batted ball, heading straight for the cow. He leaped for the whipping tail and as soon as Crazy Feet grabbed on, the gigantic cow shivered its hide and swung him like Tarzan, pinwheeling him through

the air back across left garden. He soared
faster than he'd ever moved (and consider-
ing how fast he ran to begin with, that was
mighty fast). The tail propelled him straight
for the cranks reaching out over the foul line
in the far left field corner.

Would the spectators clear out of the way? Would they interfere?

Crazy Feet extended his leather into the sea of hats, cups, hands, and umbrellas.

Somehow, miraculously, the ball found his mitt. A circus catch. Three hands dead!

| | 1 | 2 | 3 | 4 | 5 | 6 | 7 | 8 | 9 | R |
|---|---|---|---|---|---|---|---|---|---|---|
| CN | 0 | 3 | 3 | 0 | 0 | 0 | 4 | 7 | | 11 7 |
| TN | 6 | 1 | 1 | 4 | 5 | 6 | 0 | | | 2 3 |

# 16

★

## Beware the Cow that Kicks

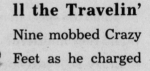

ll the Travelin'
Nine mobbed Crazy
Feet as he charged
from the field. Even Griffith, Ruby, and
Graham ran over to the edge of the rope
behind the bench to congratulate the left
scout on his brilliant grab.

Out in center garden, the cow stood still
yet again. Her tail no longer whipped; only
her cowbell swayed ever so slightly each
time she stuck up her nose and sniffed the
downtown air.

Griffith wiped the rain from his face

as he led his brother and sister back over to the crate. With Professor Lance making his way to the plate to lead off the last half of the eighth, Griffith searched the faces in the crowd one more time. At any moment, the Chancellor's men could *attack*. There were less than two innings left in the game. Why hadn't they shown themselves yet?

"Maybe we should try using the ball again," Ruby suggested.

"It couldn't hurt," Griffith answered.

But even with all three hands cautiously clutching the baseball and aiming it in the direction of the dish, the Rough Riders still couldn't hit a lick. The Professor flied out, Doc grounded out, and Guy struck out.

The Travelin' Nine headed to the final frame clinging to a six-run lead.

*Clinging.*

Happy couldn't make it back onto the field. He could barely even sit upright.

"Don't worry, Happy," Graham said. He walked behind the bench, leaned over the rope, and placed his hands gently upon the hurler's sagging shoulders. "The Travelin' Nine will take care of business."

"Son, without a doubt," Happy said. "Without a doubt."

Griffith hurried over to his brother. For a fleeting instant, he allowed the thought of Graham playing in Happy's place to enter his head, but he quickly dismissed it. Clearly, Happy did not belong out on a baseball field, but Graham wasn't the answer. The Travelin' Nine would have to make do with only eight ballists.

Trailing by six tallies, the Chicago Nine was more than willing to allow the barnstormers to take the field shorthanded. They were also pleased to see Scribe heading back out to the hill.

"We need to get back to Ruby," Griffith said as Scribe threw his last warm-up toss. "We shouldn't leave her alone."

They hustled away.

"Thirty-one," Graham said when they reached her.

"What'd you say that for?" Ruby asked.

"I had another idea."

"Let's hear it," Griffith said.

"I've been thinking about the number three and the number one," he explained. "We place three hands on one baseball. There are three of us, and we're one family. And we're three outs and one inning away from a win. Three for one and one for all."

"That's great, Grams," Ruby said. "But how's that supposed to help us or the Travelin' Nine?"

"I'm not sure." Graham shrugged. "But I

was thinking about what Daddy used to tell us about teamwork and teammates."

"Baseball is a team game," Ruby said, repeating their father's phrase. "No one player can accomplish much without the help of teammates."

Like she had so many times already this afternoon, Ruby pulled her brothers closer as they prepared to hold the baseball. She covered the ball with Griffith's shirttails, and then all three joined hands for the final frame. She peered out at the quiet cow while placing her pinky inside the hole. Then Ruby carefully lifted their hands and extended them out toward center garden.

*Moo! Moo!*

The cow's deafening call reverberated off the downtown buildings. The Travelin' Nine covered their ears. Griffith, Ruby, and Graham all wanted to block out the sound,

but instead they clutched the warming baseball and one another as tightly as ever.

The bovine began rolling her head, first
slowly, then more violently. The carriage-
size cowbell, which hung from a collar
larger than a circus ring, swung back and
forth.

"What's happening?" Graham asked.

"What did we just do?" Ruby added.

Suddenly, the cow lifted her back legs one
at a time and kicked out her hooves like she
was preparing to charge.

*Stomp! Stomp! Stomp!*

The mammoth cow began to move. She
headed straight for Tales.

"Do something!" Graham shouted at his
brother.

"Like what?" Griffith answered.

Without warning, the bovine raised her
right front hoof and kicked at Tales. The
Travelin' Nine's second sack man leaped out

The bovine . . . kicked at Tales.

of the way, tumbling into short right garden.

"Beware the cow that kicks!" Griffith, Ruby, and Graham shouted as one.

Tales didn't remain on the ground for long because the cow wasn't finished.

"Look out!" the three Paynes shouted.

Once again she lifted her right front hoof and kicked at Tales. The bovine's boot narrowly missed his head as he dove back onto the infield dirt. Rolling across the diamond, Tales scrambled to his feet by the pitcher's hill, where he stood shoulder-to-hip with Scribe.

"I got it!" Griffith exclaimed, leaping as high as he could. "Tales needs to pitch."

"That's what the cow is signaling," Ruby added.

"Yes!" Graham cheered.

Griffith glanced around. Even with the Chancellor's men somewhere nearby, he had to risk it. He *needed* to tell Tales. Griffith exhaled a long breath and charged onto the field.

"Young man!" the umpire erupted. "Get off this field!"

Clearly the umpire was at his wit's end. This was the second time a child had run onto his field and interrupted his game. And what made matters worse was the additional delay that had just taken place. While the cow had caused the commotion, the umpire and Chicagolanders had not seen anything, only a team of out-of-towners behaving in a less-than-gentlemanly manner again. So it seemed.

But Griffith ignored the umpire's hollers and raced up to Tales.

"You need to pitch," Griffith said.

"I'm coming in for Scribe?" Tales twitched his bushy mustache.

"Yessir." Griffith took the ball from Scribe, pointed him to second sack, and then looked back at Tales. "You ready?"

"They don't call me Old Rough and Ready for nothing."

"Men, this is your last warning," the umpired barked when he reached the mound. "This is your last meeting of any kind." He turned to Griffith. "Young'un, I'm not going to say it again. Get off this green oasis!"

Griffith looked up. For the entire mound meeting, the bovine had hovered over the ballists. She no longer kicked or mooed; she just stood there, and from time to time, nodded. As if she were listening. Now, at the end of the conversation, the large cow looked straight at Griffith. Griffith stared back, and while he wasn't absolutely certain, he could've sworn he saw the cow *wink*.

Hightailing from the field, Griffith rejoined his brother and sister and immediately placed his hand back on the ball. And at the very moment all three hands landed in their familiar places on the baseball, Mrs. O'Leary's cow disappeared.

# 17

★

## Tales Takes His Turn

s soon as **Tales** toed the rubber, Griffith realized the second bag man was indeed the right reliever. His constant chatter was going to drive the Chicago Nine strikers batty.

"Who is he talking to?" Graham asked as he watched Tales's bushy mustache flap up and down.

"You know how he is," Ruby replied. "Tales likes to call the action and do the play-by-play when he's out on the field."

"Well, let's just hope the talking mustache

doesn't describe the pitches before he throws them!" Griffith exclaimed.

*Then again,* Griffith thought, *it might not make much of a difference if he did.* Tales didn't have an accurate arm. Sure, he could make the throw from second to first with the best of them, but that was it. That's why Tales was such an unlikely substitute. It was also the reason Griffith hadn't even considered him as a replacement for Happy in the first place.

At most, Tales was good for one inning. His loose lips would—hopefully—distract them for that long. After that, the Chicago Nine were bound to realize he couldn't pitch the ball over the plate.

Tales peered in at the target Guy held out behind the dish. "Around comes the arm," Tales announced, "and here comes the pitch."

In Happy-like fashion, he started the first Chicago striker off with an over-the-top fastball.

"Ball one!"

Graham looked to his brother and sister. "It wasn't on fire."

"It wasn't even close," Ruby added.

"Don't worry," Griffith said. "I'm positive the cow was telling us that Tales is our man."

"The pitcher sets." Tales continued with his call. "He reads the backstop's signs, nods his head, and rocks into his motion."

SLURVE:
*pitch that contains qualities of both slider and curveball.*

BALTIMORE CHOP:
*ground ball that hits in front of home plate (or off of it) and takes a large bounce, sometimes (but not always) over an infielder's head.*

For his second offering, Tales threw a sidearm slurve that was even farther off the plate than the first pitch. But the Chicago striker was so baffled by Tales's babble, he swung mightily anyway. The batter drove the ball into the ground, a Baltimore chop toward first. Professor Lance charged the high-bounding grounder. He fielded it bare-handed, slid to a stop, side-turned, and lunged for the runner. He tagged the runner's foot a millisecond before it landed on the bag.

"Yer out!" cried the umpire.

One hand down. As he returned to the hill, Tales recounted (out loud) every last detail of the Professor's stellar defensive play. Listening to the talking mustache, the Chicago Nine's next batter grew impatient. By the time Tales threw his first pitch— one of Happy's between-the-legs specials that soared way out of the strike zone—the striker was swinging no matter what.

Lunging wildly for the offering, the Chicago striker managed to stroke a daisy cutter destined for the hole between short-stop and third. Doc dove for the ball. It tipped off his leather and bounded toward Bubbles, who had broken toward third on contact. Bubbles gloved the ball back-handed, leaped into the air, and fired the pill across his body and the diamond. The professor stretched for the throw, but it didn't reach. The short-hop skidded off his

"Just like at practice!"

glove . . . in the direction of Scribe, who had been backing up the play. Only a man of Scribe's size had any chance of snaring the ball. Extending his large, bare hand as far as he could, Scribe grabbed the pill and stomped the bag.

"Out!" the umpire called.

Two hands down.

"Just like at practice!" Graham exclaimed.

Scribe tipped his cap in the direction of the Paynes.

Then Graham repeated Woody's words from yesterday (without his drawl, of course). "That's what practice is all about. I reckon that's what it means to be part of a team."

Tales stepped back to the pitcher's hill, and once again he started calling the play-by-play.

"It all comes down to this," he announced. "Two down, top of the last, home team trails by six. Ace reliever Zachary Tales Taylor sizes up his target. He shakes off one set of signs. And another. And still another. Now he's set. He rocks into motion. Here's the windup and now the pitch."

The Chicago Nine's frustrated batter swung at a ball two feet over his head. He *blasted* it, but the wind off the lake propelled the rock straight into the air like a rocket.

"I got it!" Guy called.

She danced under the towering pop-up. Then, at the very instant the ball reached its highest point, the first rays of sunshine peeked out from behind the skies of gray. Guy shielded her eyes with her mitt as she followed the flight of the baseball . . . until it landed in her glove with a gentle pop.

"Third hand dead!" the umpire declared. "The Travelin' Nine win!"

Ruby and Graham stormed the field, but at that moment of jubilation, Griffith hesitated. For a second, his thoughts leaped to the Chancellor and his men. What had happened to them? There had to have been a reason they didn't show. What had he missed?

However, Griffith's head remained there for only that second. He quickly followed after his brother and sister, joining them as they piled atop their mother, who still held the final out high above her head.

But the other members of the Travelin' Nine did not join the home plate celebration. Instead, they raced toward the bench. Happy had slumped over and lay facedown on the ground.

# 18

★

*Back at the Inn*

**R**uby dabbed Happy's neck and cheeks with the damp cloth and then gently placed it back on his forehead.

"Is that what Daddy would've looked like?" Graham asked.

"No," Ruby responded instantly. "That's not what he would have looked like."

But she couldn't blame him for asking. Graham hadn't seen their father at the funeral. None of them had. After the accident on the bay, their father's body was never recovered. For days, dozens of fishing boats had combed the waters off Annapolis, but to no avail. On that scorching July afternoon a little over a month ago, they had lowered an empty casket into the earth.

"Happy's very much alive." Ruby placed both hands upon her brother's shoulders. "He's not going anywhere."

Only a couple of hours earlier, the Travelin' Nine had carried Happy off the field like a soldier wounded in battle. For what had seemed like an eternity, he didn't move or even open his eyes.

But after arriving back at the inn, he had started showing signs of life. He'd even insisted the barnstormers wheel his cot into the parlor so he could be present for the team meeting. At first, the ballists had refused; they wanted Happy to rest. However, the stubborn old-timer refused to relent. So they compromised. Happy could join the others if he promised to remain lying down and silent. For the most part, Happy had adhered to the bargain, but every so often he would sit up, hold his own cup of tea, and attempt to participate in the postgame party.

Yes, the Travelin' Nine still celebrated their victory, and they had the hometown ballists to thank for that. In an admirable display of sportsmanship and camaraderie, the Chicago Nine had collected some of the food from the field and brought it back to the inn. Since they had planned on serving a new American sandwich called the hamburger, they were easily able to transport more than enough to feed a small army (which the Rough Riders were).

Still, Ruby and her brothers had found it difficult to celebrate because of the news about Happy. His playing days were over. *Both* of the doctors who examined him had made that perfectly clear. Happy had been trying to do way too much for way too long, and it had finally caught up with him. His weakened heart could no longer handle the stress and strain of the travel and ball playing. If he didn't slow down immediately, there was a chance he could die.

Ruby looked over at Professor Lance, who had stepped to the front of the room. He would be presiding over the meeting today in place of Happy. Ruby pointed Graham to an empty chair by the door next to Tales, and then she sat down beside Scribe on the parlor floor at the foot of Happy's cot. She flipped to a blank page in her journal, placed it in her lap, and prepared to take notes.

"Let's start with the good news," Professor Lance said. He lifted a box off the shelf behind him and tilted it so that everyone could see the contents.

"Huzzah!" the barnstormers toasted.

The box was filled with hundreds and hundreds of dollars worth of coins and bills. Not only had the Travelin' Nine raised far more money than they had in Louisville, but they had also more than made up for the money

**"HUZZAH!":** *common cheer to show appreciation for a team's effort.*

179

they didn't earn in Cincinnati. In their possession they now had $625.

The Professor returned the box to the shelf and faced his teammates again. Now he wore a stoic expression.

"Gentlemen, we are confronted with many questions," he began. "How do we continue playing without Happy? Will teams play against us if we cannot field a full nine?"

Silence.

"Do we need to find a replacement? Can anyone replace Happy?"

More silence.

"These strange events that continue to assist us—the ones these children are using to help guide us to victory—can we expect them to continue if one of us is unable? Will they occur if our circle is broken?"

For several hours, Griffith, Ruby, Graham, and all the Travelin' Nine remained in the parlor. One by one, they went through the Professor's questions.

The Rough Riders unanimously agreed to forge ahead. Not that Happy would've permitted them to pursue an alternative course.

"I may not be able to play," he managed to mutter, "but there is no *I* in the word 'team.' Nor is there an *I* in 'barnstormers.' This show goes on."

They were the first words Happy said all meeting, and once he spoke them, everyone felt things were going to somehow work out—though at the moment, they didn't exactly know how.

A replacement ballist was needed.

However, the team could not agree on the way to find one.

"How 'bout that Evers lad?" Woody suggested. "Remember them plays he made back in the third? He was quite the gloveman out there. I reckon we should see if he'd consider travelin' to the north country with us."

Tales didn't like the idea. "We already have a second sack man," he said, pointing to himself. "What we need is a hurler."

Doc Lindy didn't like Woody's proposal either, but for a different reason. He believed that the replacement ballist needed to be a Rough Rider.

"How on earth are we going to find another Rough Rider who plays baseball?" the Professor asked. "The only ones who do are gathered right here in this room."

Doc didn't have an answer.

"I know what we have to do," Graham announced. "It's obvious."

All eyes turned to the youngest person

in the room. He held a train schedule and map in one hand, and his fourth hearty hamburger in the other. Everyone waited for him to finish chewing.

"We must catch our train," he said. "We already have the tickets, and it would be too expensive to buy new ones."

The ballists nodded.

"Minneapolis is a big city," Graham continued. "It may not be as big as Chicago, but I'm sure we'd find players willing to join us for practice. We can hold tryouts. Griffith, Ruby, and I can be your scouts." He motioned to his brother and sister. "We're excellent judges of talent. Especially Griffith. We'll find you a new player."

"Brilliant!" Bubbles declared. "Minneapolis is known for producing some of the finest young baseball talent in all the heartland."

"Really?" Ruby eyed him sideways.

Bubbles scratched what remained of his

left ear. "As a matter of fact, if you're raised in Minnesota, once you're able to walk, they hand you a ball and bat."

"Are you sure?"

Bubbles nodded emphatically. "My uncle's cousin's brother-in-law is from those parts, and he says—"

"Is that the truth?" Ruby interrupted.

"I think so," Bubbles replied. "Well, maybe." He thought some more. "Let's just say it could be."

"Where did that come from?" Griffith asked, tousling Graham's hair.

"Where did what come from?"

"All those great ideas," Griffith replied. "Since when did you get to be so smart?"

Graham shrugged.

"I must be rubbing off on you," Griffith said, patting his chest.

Graham dismissed his brother with the wave of a hand. "Keep telling yourself that."

# 19

★

## *The Encounter*

**riffith clutched** the pillow behind his neck and peeked over at Ruby and Graham. Both slept soundly in their beds. He let out a long, exasperated puff. Once again he couldn't sleep, nor would he any time soon.

At the game, and then for most of the evening, Griffith had been concerned about Happy, just like everyone else. And just like everyone else, he had been relieved to learn from the physicians that Happy was going to be okay, so long as he didn't play and got plenty of rest. All the barnstormers would see to it that he obeyed the doctors' orders.

But now, in the solitude of night, Griffith's rapid-fire thoughts had turned to the Chancellor and his men. There had been no sign of them—not before the game, not during, not after. The more Griffith thought about it, the less sense it made. In many ways, Griffith was more frightened by having *not* seen them.

Staying in bed was making things worse. He let out another long breath and shook his head. It was only a matter of time before his uneasy feelings turned to panic. He needed fresh air. Now.

Griffith took the lantern from the end table and climbed out of bed. After glancing one last time at his sleeping siblings, he slipped on some clothes before tiptoeing from the room and down the three flights of stairs. Then he opened the screen door and sat on the stoop. Placing the lantern by his feet, he faced the sleeping city.

Chicago was a different place in the middle of the night. During the day, the streets were filled with pedestrians and trains, peddlers and trolleys. It was louder than a Fourth of July parade. But right now, Chicagoland slept.

He wrapped his arms across his chest and slowly rocked to and fro. Griffith had hoped that being outside would calm him, but it didn't. Sitting alone in the dark, he felt even more anxious. Vulnerable.

The city was silent, except for the low rumble coming from a lone motorcar idling at the corner. A small group of men was gathered beside it. Griffith looked their way. A single figure began walking up the sidewalk in his direction. It was so quiet that Griffith could hear the click of the man's soles on the pavement.

Griffith reached for the lantern. He

grabbed the handle and tilted the light toward the——-

"Look who we have here."

The voice startled Griffith, and he fumbled the lantern. It crashed to the steps. The glass shattered, extinguishing the flame.

Griffith looked up. The man who had been walking up the block now stood on the sidewalk in front of him.

"Little boy," the man said, "I couldn't have scripted our first encounter any better."

The light from the lamppost cast a shadow across the man. Griffith could only make out part of his face, but he didn't need to see any more of his sunken features to know exactly who the man was.

"Little boy, do you not speak?" the man asked, his raspy voice growing louder.

Griffith sat up taller, but did not answer.

The man took a step toward Griffith. "You may think your Rough Rider friends can protect you," he said, pulling the brim of his hat down farther over his eyes, "but no one can. Nothing will."

Griffith swallowed. With the man hovering over him, Griffith felt the bile rise up his throat. An acidic taste pooled in the back of his mouth.

"Little boy," the man continued, "I know you've been told I always get what I want. I want that baseball. But . . ." He paused. Then he leaned in even closer. "That's not all I want. You have something else that I want too."

Griffith's opened his mouth to breathe, but the terror blocked his airway.

"And just so you know," the man said, straightening. He took a step away, and then pointed two disfigured fingers at Griffith's eyes. "Before you get any ideas, *Griffith Payne*, before you think about doing something brave, remember this: I have something *you* want."

Griffith's chest tightened. He blinked hard. A single teardrop squeezed from his left eye.

"Oh, that's right, *Griffith Payne*. I do." The man smiled, then he added, "In fact, I have *more* than one thing you want."

The Chancellor pivoted on a heel and began strolling back down the street. When he neared the men at the corner, they stopped talking and stood tall. One opened the back door of the parked motorcar for the Chancellor and shut it behind him after he stepped in. As soon as the door closed, another motorcar turned the corner and stopped. All the Chancellor's men quickly piled in.

Both vehicles sped off.

Griffith dashed inside. He charged up the stairs two at a time, stumbling twice in the pitch dark.

*I have something* you *want. Oh, that's right,* Griffith Payne. *I do.*

"You have something else that I want too."

He reached the third floor and tore down the corridor. Up ahead, the door to the bedroom where his sister and brother slept was ajar. Had he left it that way? Or had someone else?

He burst into the room. Ruby and Graham were still there, sleeping as soundly as ever.

Griffith dropped to his knees and placed a hand over his mouth. He could breathe again. The Chancellor hadn't done anything to them.

But the Chancellor knew who he was. He even knew his name. He knew about the baseball, too, and he was determined to get it. Slumping to the floor, Griffith put down the lantern and buried his face in his hands. The Chancellor also wanted something else. What could it be? And what could the Chancellor possibly have that he wanted?

# 20

★

## "Where Could She Be?"

here's Ruby?" Elizabeth's voice was filled with panic. She stood at the entrance to the train station. "Where is she?"

Next to his mother, Griffith held his head as he looked up the block. Ruby had been with them when they'd arrived. He had just seen her in front of the ticket office with Scribe and Tales. But now she was nowhere to be found.

"Where could she be?" Elizabeth raced back toward the train again and joined the other members of the Travelin' Nine as they searched the platform.

Griffith felt the nausea begin to build in the pit of his stomach, just like it had only hours before during his encounter with the Chancellor. He was still reeling—still trembling—from that meeting. No one else knew about what had happened with the Chancellor. Not yet, anyway. Griffith had planned on telling Ruby the first chance he had on the train.

But now she was missing. Could the Chancellor have something to do with her disappearance? Could—

"All aboard!" the conductor called.

Griffith whirled around. They needed to be on this train to Minneapolis, but no one even considered boarding without Ruby. The barnstormers continued to comb the depot.

"We're missing it!" Graham raced up to

Griffith. He pointed at the train. "Where is she, Griff?"

"Don't worry, Grammy," Griffith said, draping an arm over his brother's shoulder. "Everything's going to be okay."

"You don't know that," Graham replied.

No, he didn't. Griffith turned from the train. He couldn't bear to watch, but he couldn't avoid hearing—the slowly accelerating chugs of the wheels and the hooting whistle piercing the dawn—the sounds of the departing train, the sounds of opportunity lost.

Now Griffith heard something else: in his head, the Chancellor's words from a short time ago:

*That's not all I want. You have something else that I want too.*

"How can you be so sure?" Graham asked, reaching for his big brother's hand.

"It will," Griffith assured him, squeezing Graham's hand. "You'll see."

"Where is she, Griff?"

But at that moment, even Griffith didn't believe his words. This was so unlike Ruby. She would never wander off without telling someone. Something was wrong. Terribly wrong.

And to make things even worse—if that were possible—wherever she was, Ruby had the baseball.

★

*See what's on deck!*

Read a chapter from the Travelin' Nine's

next game in

# WATER, WATER
# EVERYWHERE,

AVAILABLE NOW!

★

# Preacher Wil Takes the Hill

**Preacher Wil reached under his col-**
lar for his necklace. He twirled the charm in
his fingers and kissed it gently before tuck-
ing it back in. Then he stepped forth from
the dugout, and for the first time in many,
many years, he headed to the hill to pitch in
a baseball game.

**HILL:**
*pitcher's mound.*
*Also called*
*"bump"*

From half a field away, through the slats in
the outfield fence, Ruby could see the pride
on his face. She smiled wide.

But as Preacher Wil crossed over the foul
line and into fair territory, the raging-river
sound grew louder.

"I don't like what I'm hearing," Griffith said.

Neither did Ruby. With each step Preacher Wil took toward the mound, the din of roaring rapids rose until it hit almost eardrum-piercing levels. Some of the Travelin' Nine covered their ears (though Bubbles only covered what remained of his left one). However, the Millers and their cranks didn't because they couldn't hear a thing.

When Preacher Wil reached the rubber, the surface of the field began to crack. Water surged in, and for a moment the pitcher's mound became an island. In a matter of seconds a chasm opened up, and the water rushed into it, slicing a divide across the entire pitch. The waterway started by the Millers' dugout, cut through the infield between Tales and second sack, and swung back to the outer garden wall. Professor, Tales, and Woody stood on one side of the

**FOUL LINES:** *lines extending from home plate through first and third base and all the way to the outfield. Anything within the lines is considered to be in fair territory; anything outside the lines is in foul territory.*

river, while the rest of the Rough Riders were on the other.

"Look at the way it's divided the barn-stormers." Ruby pointed. "The three players who voted against Preacher Wil because of his skin color are separated from the rest of the team."

"How did you see that so fast?" asked Griffith.

"That's easy, Griff," Graham answered first. "Your little sister is smarter than you!"

Griffith elbowed Graham. "And my little brother is about to get sat on!"

"Only we can see this," Ruby noted, directing her brothers' eyes to the Millers' dugout and the cranks seated behind it. None of the locals were reacting to the new on-field obstacle.

"How are the barnstormers going to play with a river running through the field?" Graham asked.

The stream was far too wide for the ballists to hurdle, and even though it was level, the fast-moving, rushing rapids made it unsafe for swimming. If a batted ball or throw happened to land in the water, the ballists would have to wait for the currents to carry it ashore.

Ruby frowned. "I have a feeling this is just the beginning."

She faced the mound again and noticed that Preacher Wil had *transformed*. Firing his warm-up tosses to Guy, he no longer looked like the kind and gentle man she had come to know these last few days. His welcoming smile and soothing eyes had vanished. Preacher Wil now looked like a warrior.

"Good," Ruby whispered to herself. "That's exactly what the Travelin' Nine need."

Preacher Wil stared down Germany Smith, the Minneapolis Millers' leadoff striker. Then he peered in at Guy's target, dipped his left hand into his mitt, and gripped the pill. Finally he raised his arms high over his head, pivoted into his windup, and fired the first pitch.

All Smith could do was watch the perfect fastball sail right over the heart of home dish.

But the umpire failed to lift his right fist and signal a strike. Instead, both hands remained on his knees.

Griffith, Ruby, Graham, and the barnstormers wanted to question the umpire's call; however, everyone knew better than to challenge his authority. Once an umpire issued a ruling, there was never a debate.

For his next offering, Preacher Wil threw a fluttering curveball, a pitch even more perfect than his first—if that were possible. And for the second time in a row, all Germany

Smith could do was watch it cross the plate.

Yet once again, the umpire didn't rise out of his crouch behind the dish to indicate a strike.

"Where was it?" Graham asked.

"That's what I'd like to know," replied Griffith.

Graham pounded his leg with a fist. "That umpire shouldn't be wearing a top hat and tails. He should be wearing a Millers uniform."

"Daddy always told us never to disagree with an umpire," Ruby grumbled, "but it's impossible to agree with this one."

The three Paynes realized they were up against a force they had no control over. All the calls—close and not so close—were going in favor of the home team. It was like the Millers were playing with ten ballists.

Preacher Wil had to realize it too, but his mound manner didn't change.

Germany Smith took Preacher Wil's next two pitches as well, and on four straight *strikes*, the Millers had their leadoff man on.

"He can't find the plate!" a row of rooters began to chant.

"Anyone have a map?" shouted a fan. "Pitcher needs directions to the dish!"

"The southpaw needs glasses!" another chorus of cranks sang.

And others called out even worse insults— ones that mocked Preacher Wil's skin color.

Griffith grabbed the back of his neck. Listening to the cries of the locals, he was reminded of the conversations he used to have with his father when they played catch in the yard. His father would lament how baseball had changed. It used to be a gentlemen's sport, but because it had grown rapidly, it had acquired an edge, an edge his father could not accept or understand.

In spite of the umpire's calls and the

**SOUTHPAW:** left-handed individual; the commonly used nickname for players who throw left-handed.

fans' behavior, Preacher Wil didn't so much as flinch. He simply kept on pitching.

The Millers' next batter took the first two pitches, both strikes that were called balls. Ahead in the count, he swung at the third offering, grounding a grass clipper to Bubbles at shortstop, a surefire double-play ball. However, in order to cover the sack, Tales had to cross the stream. He instinctively broke for the bag, but then realized the water was in the way. Screeching to a halt, he teetered along the shore like a tightrope walker struggling to keep his balance. With Tales trying not to topple, Bubbles's only play was to first.

*Splash!*

To the Minneapolitans, it seemed like Bubbles didn't know how to force out a base runner. They had no idea what to make of Tales, either. He was lying facedown on the infield dirt, kicking his arms and legs like a

**GRASS CLIPPER:** *ground ball. Also known as "daisy cutter" or "bug bruiser".*

**BAG:** *base. Also called "sack".*

baby (though he was really battling the current). Then, when he climbed back onto dry land and began wringing out his clothes, the locals thought he had truly lost his marbles.

"We need to get rid of that river." Graham waved at the waterway. "They can't make plays."

"I don't think that river's going anywhere," Ruby stated.

"What makes you say that?" asked Graham.

"As long as the Travelin' Nine are divided," she said, shaking her head, "that field's going to be divided."

The next batter, the Millers' strapping young catcher, Roger Bresnahan, smacked a sky ball to right. Ordinarily it would have been an easy catch for Woody. However, because of what had happened on the previous play, the Travelin Nine's right scout didn't race after the rawhide. Stopping a few strides short of the stream, he waited for the splash landing. Then he plucked the ball from the water and shook it out before firing it back in to the cutoff man. By that time Germany Smith had scored from second, and the Millers had the early lead.

"Hang in there, Preacher Wil," Ruby whispered. "Hang in there."

As frustrated as she was by the unfair umpire, the unruly cranks, and the divided diamond, Ruby refused to lose hope. For one thing, the hometown hitters were swinging the timber and looking to put the ball in play. So long as they were, the Travelin' Nine had a chance to record outs.

Preacher Wil was the other reason for hope. He was more than maintaining his poise and holding his own on the hill. The next striker, Jack Menefee, skied to Scribe in center for out number two, and Bresnahan was unable to advance from second sack.

**CUTOFF MAN:**
*infielder who catches a throw from an outfielder in an attempt to hold up a base runner who is heading for a base or home plate or to help a ball get to its intended target faster.*

**DIAMOND:**
*infield.*

**TIMBER:**
*baseball bat. Also called "lumber".*

**SKY (v.):**
*to hit a fly ball.*

Then Perry Werden hit a liner up the middle that Preacher Wil plucked from the air with his bare hand to close out the frame.

"It could've been worse," Griffith noted.

"A lot worse," added Ruby.

"They only got one," Graham pointed out. "Now we need to figure out how to get that river to disappear."

All of a sudden, that's what started to occur. As Preacher Wil stepped from the hill and the players began leaving the pitch, the waters slowed and the river narrowed. By the time the Travelin' Nine had reached the dugout and the Millers had retaken the field, not a single drop of water remained.

"It's gone!" Graham announced.

"And so are we," Griffith said, letting go of the baseball.

"What do you mean?" asked Graham.

Ruby knew exactly what Griffith meant. As perfect a hiding spot as this was, it was only a matter of time until they were discovered. And she was certain Griffith had seen the ushers searching the bleachers not far from where they stood, just like she had. One inning in the same spot was long enough. Ruby needed to find their next safe lookout.

"Follow me, boys!"